Table of Content

Heart's bonds

Heart's bonds

Heart's bonds

Heart's bonds

Heart's bonds

Novel

Pascale d'Harmat

English translation :
Agnès Rouvrais-Waysbaum

Artwork and pictures: Marie-Christine Lambert,
Artistique Director

Heart's bonds

Editions Claire Fontaine
6, rue des petits champs
78360 Montesson
Siret 503 978 702 000 10
www.editions-claire-fontaine.com
contact@editions-claire-fontaine.com

ISBN 978-2-917734-60-5

Novel

This is a novel; any resemblance with existing characters today or in the past, can only be unintentional and of pure coincidence.

For all the children victims of wars and for all of those who come to their rescue.
Pascale d'Harmat,
Montesson, July 1st 2011

"Whatever you did for one of the least of these brothers and sisters of mine, you did it for me."
Gospel, Mat (25, 40-41)

TABLE OF CONTENTS

Table of Content

PART I

Heart's bonds

Heart's bonds

USA Embassy, Saigon, April 29, 1975

- Thank you, Bert.

With a sad smile, Lich puts in his pockets the passports with visas, which his friend has obtained for him. They represent a 'life certificate' in the middle of the rout of the American and South Vietnamese armies after the progress of the Viet Ming troops. They listen to the news on the radio:

'Since Phuoc Long capitulated after fighting for ten days, general Van Tien army gained the little town of Ban Me Thuot on the high plateau of the centre of the country. It is obvious that the Americans want to leave as soon as possible, the road is almost clear and the troops from Hanoi are marching to Saigon. General Van Tien Dung skilfully managed to make believe that he was going to attack two other high plateaus, Pleiku and Kontum. As a result, since Ban Me Thuot fell too, a wind of panic is blowing among the South Vietnamese Generals; the withdrawal has become a disastrous escape to the coasts. Van Tien Dung is the master of the high plateau in Vietnam, as we always say: 'whoever controls the high plateau, controls the country.'

Since the end of March, the lines of trucks of the army of the North have entered Da-Nang, eliminating the best troops of the South Vietnamese Army, opening the road to Saigon, today they arrive…'

Bert is very nervous; he is shaking his friend a bit, calling him by his Americanized name:
'Lee, I'm telling you again, hurry, the air lift has begun and we have received the order to start evacuating the American citizens, then our Vietnamese friends. I managed to have a high priority status for

you and your family, because you are like my brother, but I cannot guarantee you that everything will be fine. Tension will rise and things may not go as planned. Our men are at a breaking point. Do not wait one more hour; the evacuation is going to start.'

'I go get my wife and my son and I will be back as soon as possible.'

'There are Viet Ming shooters in the city, the streets are not safe. Wait, I am going to find a jeep and a guard. Pay attention, when the radio plays 'White Christmas,' it will be the signal to go to the Embassy. Try to be there before, because we may very well be overwhelmed. I may very well not be there when you come back: see you in Beverly Hills, I will be waiting for you with a bottle of Champagne, you will see, you will love the American way of life!

Bert gives him a hug, leaves him in Sergeant Bob Dyane's care, and goes without turning back.

Bert Codman, architect, joined the army and received an engineer education, convinced that he had to 'free Vietnam', just like his father and grandfather had 'freed France' before him. However what he found when he arrived was a completely different situation, which only kept deteriorating.

The North has never recognized the Nguyen Van Thieu regime, supported by the United States. The Paris Peace agreements signed in 1973 tried to reconcile the country. However, for the Ho Chi Minh troops, the reunification of the country can only be achieved through war. According to him: 'the enemies and traitors will know no pity.'

The United States has strongly weakened after the Watergate issue and Richard Nixon leaving. The American public opinion is increasingly against the war; in 1975, the Congress reduced substantially the military funding to the South Vietnamese regime and does not allow any new bombarding. Since several months,

Henry Kissinger has been pressuring the Soviet Union to stop the North Vietnamese army, or at least, to make the evacuation easier for the Americans and their Vietnamese friends. Today, April 29th, it is the rout.

After three years in Vietnam, Bert had only one wish: go back home, forget about hell, and take his place again in his father's architect firm.

Two years ago, he and Nguyen Trân Lich, a young Vietnamese architect, became friends. One evening, they had drunk a little too much with friends, and the pub they were in became the target of one of the numerous attacks against GIs. Lich had the self-control to catch the grenade and throw it with all his might, thus saving the lives of the group of engineers. Since this accomplishment, Bert 'adopted' the young Vietnamese like a brother. He planned to bring him to the US as a partner at the end of his military assignment. He had not imagined that his wish would be granted beforehand, due to the terrible situation of the US troops retreat.

Sergeant Bob Dayne sidles in the streets in turmoil. Suddenly, gunfire hits the jeep and John, the soldier next to Bob, collapses. The radio plays White Christmas.

'Shit, we have to go back.'

'My wife and my son, screams Lich, you received the order to go get them!'

'Go to hell! John is hurt and if we don't go back as soon as possible, there will be three corpses in the jeep.'

Bob turns around and rushes to the Embassy. When they arrive, Bob is dead. One reporter comes close and asks Bob:

- What is your impression about losing a friend so close from evacuation?

-Shit! Fucking journalist question! I only want to save my butt and that of this Viet entrusted by my officer.

He pushes the reporter away and leads Lich into the Embassy.

- My wife... she is pregnant..., my son...

Heart's bonds

The noise is at a peak, we can hear the frenzy emanating from the helicopter flights, transporting abroad diplomats, CIA agents, government VIP and anyone managing to make its way within the Embassy chaos; South Vietnamese too are trying to get in.

A few hours before Saigon was taken, the last Rangers unit in the Embassy bars the doors and find refuge on the roof. They are evacuated a few minutes later by a helicopter.

The airlift comes to an end at dawn on April 30th. At 5:40 precisely, the second last helicopter leaves the roof of the Embassy and the last one takes off two hours later with the Marines on duty aboard. More than 160,000 people were saved from the Viet Ming reprisals.

On April 30, 1975, at 5:30, the first soldiers from the 203rd armoured division of the North Vietnamese Army enter Saigon carefully, directly going to the Presidential Palace they occupy right away. This surprised the international community, which thought that Saigon would be taken on May 19th, the day Ho Chi Min had his birthday, calling the Vietminh campaign 'Uncle Ho.'

Carried, pushed, bumped into, Nguyen Trân Lich collapses on the deck of the American war ship. 'My wife, my son...' Like an obsession, these words come out of his lips for hours.

St Paul School, Saigon, April 29, 1975

In Spite of all the social work accomplished in South Vietnam by the sisters of Charity of St. Paul, the French authorities fear what the Viet Ming have intended to do to the Catholics and give them the order to evacuate. Some voluntary workers, mainly Vietnamese nuns who are also nurses choose to take a chance and stay, so that both hospitals of the congregation remain open, foreseeing an influx of injured.

Schools and orphanages are closed, children are evacuated. The majority of the French nuns have returned to Paris with their Mother Superior, who left the novice mistress in charge. Sister Marie-Claire looks with nostalgia at the room where for close to three years she has taught English and French to children hungry to learn, always smiling and so obedient compared to the young French she knew in her childhood! She is going to miss them so much... The library has been emptied from its books translated into Vietnamese by the congregation: the Gospels, the stories of the Saints, the French-Chinese-Vietnamese dictionary, children books. She closes the door. The next room is the Enamel Workshop, it has been cleared too: the crosses, the pillboxes, the decorative objects made by the children have been sent to M.E.P.* (Missions Etrangères de Paris). 'Lord, lets us come back soon...' The nun's praying is interrupted by an explosion, which makes the wall tremble. The fighting seems to come closer and closer. It is time to reach the French Embassy. A dozen nuns and novices are expected there.

-Sister Marie-Claire, come quick!

-What is going on Dao?

-There in an injured woman, just at the bus stop!

-Lord Mary Joseph!

Heart's bonds

Sister Marie-Claire hurries. The nuns are all gathered around the wounded woman; she makes her way through. There, on the ground, a young pregnant woman with a little boy lies, unconscious, with a large wound on her head.

Sister Anh is already there. She has grabbed the emergency kit and is dressing the woman. The child is not crying, he is looking at his mother and lets sister Michèle hold him.

-I gave her a morphine shot. She has lost a lot of blood, and we need to take her to the hospital.

-It is way too risky. The hospital is in the middle of the combat zone. And we should be already gone. Take her in the minibus, we will pack ourselves. Let's take her to the Embassy.

-But they will never let us evacuate her.

-Hurry, put a novice dress on her; we will say she is one of us.

- But she is pregnant! We don't even know who she is! And the child, what do we do about him?

-We will hide him easily. In any case, among the general confusion, nobody will look at us too closely. With all the troops entering the city, it is the only way to save the three of them.

Sister Marie-Claire, novice mistress, and so respectful of the rules, is unable to explain her doing, but she strongly believes that God put these unfortunate people on her path and that she is responsible for them. She knows that if she abandons them, they have no chance to survive, and if she tries to take them to the hospital, she is putting all the sisters in great danger. At that moment, nothing else matters and seeing her determination, the other sisters do as she says.

Heart's bonds

The next hours seem like a nightmare, the noise, the screaming, the flashlights, the pushing...

An eternity later, in the plane flying to France, the young woman is still unconscious, but her breathing is even. Sister Marie-Claire is holding her hand and hugging the little boy asleep.

The pilot has told the control tower that they need an ambulance to evacuate a badly injured woman. When they arrive at the airport, Le Bourget, the nun goes into the ambulance with the woman, the child and Sister Dao. A few hours later, in the intensive care unit, the woman wakes up.

-Where am I? Where is my son? My husband? What happened? She asks in Vietnamese.

Sister Marie-Claire introduces herself and explains the situation, trying to reassure her the best she can.

-What is your name?

'Little Laughing Flower.' My son is called 'Little Imperfect Thing.'

The nun is smiling. It is the custom to give a temporary name to a little child, so that gods and demons will not be jealous and will not try to take him away.

-When is the baby due?

-Any time soon. Maybe now...

-Do you have contractions?

-Yes, the baby told me to wake up.

-I am going to fetch the intern, don't worry.

The intern contacts the maternity ward, but there is no bed available. In the middle of the night, the emergency unit is already overwhelmed. It is impossible to reach a midwife.

-Sister, I have never delivered a baby and this delivery seems to be difficult, the patient has already lost a lot of blood, her wound on the head tore a part of her cranium. I don't know by which miracle she is still alive and was able to wake up.

-I was raised on a farm, we had horses and I often helped the mares give birth, I can assist you. As for miracle, that is my part!

The nun does not hesitate to wear a nurse uniform, more adapted to the circumstances. When she goes back to her protégée, the latter does not recognize her right away; she is agitated and tears run down her cheeks. The nun sponges her feverish forehead, takes her hand and sings a Vietnamese nursery rhyme.

As time goes by, it seems increasingly clear that the mother does not have the strength to give birth. In the morning, exhausted, she asks:

-Sister, I know I am going to meet my ancestors very soon, please save my baby and promise me to take care of my children until they find their father.

-I promise you.

Little Flower smiles and then dies. The medical team does not hesitate anymore: there is one chance left for the baby to live. A caesarean section is immediately done and frees the little boy, in distress, but alive.

-Two days in an incubator and he will be full of energy! Says the intern, relieved by this half-success. Thank you Sister, I don't know what I would have done without you.

The nun puts the baby, for an instant, on the dead heart of his mother, and then holds him on hers. Then she starts to take care of the new born before going to the maternity ward to put him in an incubator.

Despite her exhaustion, she insists on laying the mother's corpse and must do a lot of paperwork. She wants to treat her like one of her sisters: she will be buried in the congregation at her own expenses. She finds Sister Dao in the waiting room, the child sleeping in her arms. Sister Marie-Claire tells her what happened, in Vietnamese, not wishing to unveil the situation in a public space. Then both go find the intern.

-Doctor, I need to ask you a favor.
-Anything I can do, what do you need?
-Before dying, the mother entrusted me with her two children. I need you to be the witness.
-But I don't speak Vietnamese!
-Sister Dao will confirm.
-But she was not in the room!
-Doctor, I gave my word to this woman, before God, I swear to you that she asked me to take care of her children, I must respect my promise and the wish of a dying woman, but in the eye of the administration, my words are worth nothing if they

are not confirmed by a testimony. Otherwise, the children will be in the hands of the Welfare Services.

The intern looks at both the nun and the child. He closes his eyes. He thinks of all that happened in the last hours. The mother begging the nun, her hands, her eyes... In all honesty, did he believe that the dying woman entrusted the nun with her children? Without a doubt, any mother, being a refugee in a completely foreign country, would hang on to the person she knows and who speaks her language. Will the children be better off with the sisters than in the welfare services? It may not matter for the newborn, but for the little boy who just lost his mother, the trauma will be higher. After a long silence, choosing to follow his conscious instead of the protocol, the doctor looks at the young women and smiles:
-Alright, I am signing.

Congregation House, Chartres

May 12, 1975

- Sister Marie-Claire, do you realize what you have done? In which situation you have put us all. I would never have imagined such a scandal...

Father Benoît is furious. With over 50,000 Vietnamese refugees in France in just a few days, how will he be able to find the family of those two poor children? The young woman is dead, only giving Vietnamese names, as for the boy, he barely speaks. Only one identification sign: the bracelet he carries: 'Nguyen Trân.' Why not go look for Jack Smith in England or a needle in a haystack?

Sister Marie-Claire is waiting for the priest to finish his long monolog and his angriness to pass. Finally, he stops talking.

-I am leaving the Order. I am going to raise these children until we find their family.
-That is out of the question! We need nuns like you more than ever. We will have to take care of many orphans. The Vietnamese children are counting on you. Think of your huge responsibility. Do not let us down.

He softens up again, being the friend and confessor before the Superior and the representative of the Order. Sister Marie-Claire takes advantage of it to push her arguments.
-I promised their mother to take care of her children. God has put them in my path. He entrusted me with them...
-Nonsense, interrupts the priest. Hundreds of children have been put in your path and were in your care and thousands other are waiting for you.

-I cannot explain, this time, the nun interrupts the priest. I have never felt such a calling, I cannot ignore it.

-What is wrong, kiddo, you too have a biological clock? Is that it?

-I cannot imagine putting that child in an orphanage, neither the baby who was born in such tragic circumstances...

Both become quiet. Sometimes, the sorrow is too great, even for the Saints. After a long silence, Father Benoît offers:

-Take a few weeks off. Go to your parents with the two kids and see what can be arranged until we find their family. How old is the eldest?

-The doctor thinks he is between 30 and 36 months, according to his teeth, but he is very tiny and has suffered from the war and barely talks, which is why it is difficult to be more accurate.

The priest holds the nuns hands and looks at her in the eyes.

-Do not let us down, Marie-Claire, the Lord cannot be wishing that.

The 'Ferme Haute', June 14, 1975

A few miles from Saissac, half an hour north of Carcassonne, the 'Ferme Haute', or High Farm, received its name because of its position on a high rock, well above the castle. Built on a terrace facing the plains of Carcassonne and Malepere hills, the castle dates from 10th Century. The ruins from the surrounding walls are in a quadrilateral shape and what remains of the towers can be found at each angle. What is left of the polygonal donjon which defended the Southern slope dates back from the end of the 13th Century. The general mutilated aspect reminds of the Cathar drama and makes this place one of the typical sites of the Montagnes Noires or Black Mountain. The inhabitants of these mountains are built in rock and drama.

The vineyards produce wine with exalting aroma, smooth and deep in taste. They are called Fitou, Malepère, Quatourze, Crémant de Limoux, Muscat de Rivesaltes... The farmers raise ducks, whose foie gras* makes any celebration merry, the woods are full of boletus mushrooms and truffles and when the weather is good, one can see the white chains of the Pyrenees.

This is where Sister Marie-Claire grew up, at a time when she was still called 'Christine' and when she helped her parents in the farm, dreaming of the day when she would go far away, in the countries she learned about in geography class.

She spoke for a long time on the telephone with her mother, 'La Simone', as she is known there. She told how she had to tragically leave Saigon, the wounded woman, the birth by C-section of her second son. She did not need to talk about her love for the two orphans; her mother listened, and then simply said:

-When are you coming, so that I can prepare a room? Oh boudiou*, what have I done with the crib? You see, our Didier is about to be eleven, you will see, a real little man!

It has been almost two months now that the nun is playing the mother. She chose names for the children; it will be Pascal for the eldest, because she found him during the Easter time and Benoît for the youngest, the name of the priest, mentor and confessor of the nun. She received the authorization from the Mother Superior to have them baptized and to be their Godmother; at least this bond will last forever.

*French for fat liver is a well-known delicacy in French cuisine made of the liver of duck or goose

**Exclamation from the South of France to say «Good Lord»*

However, who would come to take away her two little treasures? Two voices are warring in her heart; the one she does not want to hear says: *"They are not yours."*

Sister Marie-Claire parks the car in the farmyard: nothing has changed. A young boy is running towards her.

-Didier, My God, you are so big!
-Quick, I want to see the pitchouns*.
- Be careful, Pascal is a little withdrawned; he does not talk and follows me around all the time.

Simone has just arrived, she holds her daughter in her arms and starts crying. Louis, the father, stays at the door; he is waiting for the women to finish their 'non-sense' and wipes one eye: "Stupid fly", he whispers, deceiving no one.

Heart's bonds

Word of affection for a child in the south of France

Didier takes Pascal in his arms and to his Godmother' surprise, he does not cry.

-I am taking him to see the ducks, the rabbits and the horses, I am sure he has never seen any!

Simone looks at the basket where Benoit is sleeping.
-Boudiou, he is so small! I have never seen one so small as that! And you say he is six weeks! *Peuchère**, poor *pitchoun*, but you do not give him anything to eat, I believe! Hey Louis, give us something to drink! Look at your daughter, she is white as death! Come on, a good shot of Blanquette de Limoux* and you will not feel tired from the journey anymore.
- Do you have many Parisians now?
-When you told us you were coming, I cancelled the reservations of the week.

**Exclamation to make a point, in the south of France

There were still rooms available at the Martinez bed and Breakfast and they were happy to take them. For three years, we have not had our Christine at home, so we can celebrate like kings.

-Mom, it has been seven years that I'm no longer Christine, but Sister Marie-Claire.

-Well, what does it matter anyway, you are still my girl!

- Hey, look!

Didier is at the front step and in his arms, Pascal is holding a little kitten and for the first time, he shows a large smile.

-Christine, can I be their godfather?

Sister Marie-Claire hugs her brother and little Pascal.

-Sorry, bro, but they have been baptized already, and Father Benoît is their godfather. However, you are going to be their big brother and defend them, which is even more important.

The nun looks away while she dries a teardrop at the corner of her eye. She has just broken her vow of obedience: her Mother Superior and the priest told her repeatedly that her family could be no substitute to the children's family, that the priority was to find their father, or grandparents, or aunts, uncles... Is that really what the Lord wants? She cannot believe it, nor accept it. Marie-Claire stands up and goes to her dad in the yard, afraid that her mother would find out about her anxiety.

Louis is at the stables. There are a dozen horses for the guests to go horse hiking. La Ferme Haute is a country bed and breakfast known for the excellent cooking of "la Simone", the amazing landscape, the warm welcome and horse riding.

Her whole childhood comes back with the mixed smell of hay and sweat... So many fond memories. Taking on an old habit, the young woman starts rubbing down the horses with great joy, forgetting momentarily her trouble.

By the evening, the family sits at the table with a very festive meal: foie gras, white kidneys with boletus, walnut cakes...

-Christine, I have been thinking and I am going to talk honestly: look at little Pascal, he has not left Didier all day. I think that he should get used to sleeping tonight in the little bed we put in your brother's bedroom.
-No, that is not possible, he cries all night! He still needs me, he needs me to talk to him in Vietnamese, and he needs me to secure him...
-Stop! It will only make him more dependent on you. I am sorry but that is very selfish, unless you have decided to leave everything and start a new life!

-You are not fair! You cannot understand what we have been through...

-I may not have been in Saigon, but your father and I have known war. Our parents have hidden people of all kind. After the war, the army came to take away the kids who lost their parents and took them to orphanages: no word of thanks, no consideration for the kids' tears, or ours, we were not even allowed to give our address. As if all of a sudden, we became unable to take care of them, when most of them had stayed with us for at least three years and nobody ever asked us if we needed anything for them. You see, although we are peasants, we know human despair as well as you do.

-Forgive me, Mother, I did not want to hurt you... This is so new for me. I have taken care of many children, but those two are a little like mine.

-Don't cry. Nobody forced you to become a nun. You are the one who wanted to become a missionary. The trouble is, when you are 18 or 20, you are all excited and do not realize what you are giving up. And once you see what you could have, it is not that easy. What do you want to do?

-Thank you for understanding me, Mother. I still need to think about it.

-Let Pascal sleep in my room, interrupts Didier. If he cries, I will console him, and if I can't, I will go get you.

-And Benoît will sleep in mine, adds Simone.

-Are you ganging up on me? Asks Marie-Claire.

Didier kisses his older sister.

-You know well how much we love you, but Mom is right, even me I can understand that.

-What about you, Dad, you don't say anything? Don't you mind having a baby in your room, crying at night?

-If we could have, with La Simone, we would not have had two kids but ten. No, baby cries do not bother me, on the con-

trary. Well, let us stop crying, take a glass
of walnut wine and let us go to bed.

Once the boys room closed, Pascal, who
went to bed without a word, starts calling:
-Didi, Didi, ca, didi, ca...
Didier gets up and comes close to the bed:
-What ca? What do you want?
-Ca, meow.
The little boy tries to imitate the cat's
meow.
-You want the cat. That's it! Hush, I am going to get him...
-Didi, Didi...
Pascal throws his arms at him; Didier cannot resist and takes the little boy in his
arms. Holding on to his precious load, he
goes hunting for the kitten, which he finds
with no difficulty, asleep on a chair in the
dining room. The little boy smiles and
holds his treasure against his heart. The kitten does not move. Didier goes back to his
room, but when he wants to put Pascal back

into bed, the little one hangs on to him with all his strength.

-Alright, you have won, you can sleep with me tonight, but it is the first and the last one.

He lies down, holding tenderly the little boy who starts sleeping right away, the cat purring against him.

In her bedroom, Sister Marie-Claire is sleeping. Tonight, she will not experience how wonderful it is to feel a little heart beat against hers, to protect a child, abandoned and trustful. Not having her two little ones near her, tears her heart away, although they are both just a few feet away and completely safe. The nun becomes aware of the great place that they have taken in her life. She felt she was called to become a nun since her early childhood; she had no doubt about her vocation until today, when two contrary desires tear her apart. The song "la Jane" crosses her mind: "*being mother of three, what for, when she is a universal mom.*"

Heart's bonds

Father Benoît and Mother Superior's words come back to her, as do the faces of the young's novices... Oh my God, why is it so hard? My love for those children is pure, selfless. What is wrong about letting my heart be full of joy when a little child comes into my arms? Be fulfilled by giving a bottle to a baby, who, without me, would not be alive? What is my sin? Pride? Selfishness? Oh Lord, give me light. Where do you need me most?

"Anyone who loves their father or mother or wife, or children more than me is not worthy of me." Is that your answer, oh Jesus? I gave you everything without knowing. You only let me know the joy of being a mother to try my love for You? My turn to follow Job and say: *"the Lord gave, and the Lord has taken away; blessed be the name of the Lord."*

In the morning, the nun has taken her decision. She will not wait until the end of her leave to go back to her Order. Tomorrow, she will be on her way to Chartres.

June 15, 1975

-Mother, you are giving us too much!
Simone filled the trunk of the car with different cans: foie gras, boletus, green beans and other products she prepared.
-That will add variety to your food. You are not alone, that will constitute one meal.
-For a regiment, for sure!

Marie-Claire smiles and affectionately kisses her mother, always so generous.
-Thanks for everything, Mom. Will you be all right with the two children and the hosts?
-Don't you worry; I can easily find help in the village. And school is over in two weeks, I can count on your brother after that.

-Is everything clear about the kids? If Social Services come, you tell them that the children were entrusted to the congregation by their mother and you are in charge of them until the father or the family is found. If you have any problem, you have Father Benoît's and Mother Superior's phone number. Write to me regularly to give me news. I will call you each time I can.

Pascal understands that Marie-Claire is leaving. He cries silently, his cheeks full of tears. The nun holds him in her arms and talks to him in Vietnamese:

-Don't cry, Little Useless Thing, your mother Little Laughing Flower is looking upon you from heaven and I too, will always be there, even if you cannot see me. I will come back; be a good boy.

Simone takes the boy in her arms and gives him a lollipop:

-At that age, no sorrow cannot be healed by sweets.

Heart's bonds

-May you be right! Goodbye now, do not forget to write!

September 1975, La Ferme Haute

My Dear daughter,

I am sorry I did not answer to your letters earlier, but you know me, I do not like to write and high season has just finished. The last Parisians are gone, we still have a few Belgians and Dutch, but we will soon have weekenders.

Didier started school again last week. You can be proud of your little Pascal, it is incredible how he has changed in just a few months. He keeps talking better every day, he is curious of everything. Now, he is starting to say whole sentences and we can understand him very well. He is as cunning as a fox and when Didier is at school, he follows Louis, who does not know how to say no any better than his son does. Fortu-

nately, the pitchoun has a good nature because with those two fools, he could have become a spoiled little brat.

He almost does not cry at night anymore, but he keeps refusing to sleep in his own bed. I have to say that your brother acts like a mother with him. Can you believe that he let his friends down last summer to take care of Pascal ? I have tears of pride in my eyes. As for the cat, which the little boy named Samaou, she acts rather like a dog. She follows him everywhere: when you see one, you see the other one.

Benoît's name suits him well. He smiles all the time! A real baby joy. Well, all the time is a figure of speech, because he does not like his bed as well. You are going to laugh, but I had to attach him to me, like an African mom, but in front so that I can see him. What could I do, boudiou, he was screaming to death as soon as I laid him down and I had work to do, peuchère! It was not easy at first but I quickly got used to it and was awarded by his smiles and his babbling.

My only concern about the two of them is that they eat like a bird. Our good doctor Lerasle keeps telling me that it is normal, that they have a small stomach, I am not that old and I raised two children who kept asking for more than they needed. When I look at pictures of you and your brother, I can see the difference. I do not want anyone to say that they do not eat enough at my house.

Well, I am talking and talking some more, but you do not give much news about yourself in your letters. You have not told us what you are doing now in Chartres. I hope you are not hiding anything bad from me. You used to have so many funny stories to tell, which is why I am a little worried. We hope you can come for Christmas, you have not been with us for one in so many years.

After three years in Vietnam, seeing the snow again, the fire in the chimney, a real Christmas tree and a beautiful Nativity scene full of Santons de Provence*, that would do you some good, and letting you celebrate Christmas with us and the little boys is the least of what your order could do. Well, you know my opinion about that, let us not keep arguing about it.

We send you lots of kisses.
Your mother

*Small hand painted nativity scene figurines made in the south of France

October 1975, Chartres

My beloved mom,

Thank you for your long letter and I am pleased to see that my godsons are doing well, in spite of the tragedy they have been through. I know you, and I know the love you are giving them, without which they could not grow up so well. Tell Didier that I am proud of him.

You are asking for news, but I have no anecdote, nor anything funny to tell. I know you do not read the paper and that the TV news does not talk much about the Vietnamese refugees in France. It may be a good thing. In this country of Human rights and secularism, one does not keep any bound with one's origins, once the French nationality granted. All the Vietnamese who arrived and have stayed here for years have been nationalized. Catholic or Buddhists, they became part of the society without questions or any form or rejection. The fact that they mainly live between themselves does not bother anyone because they can speak French, their kids usually work well in school and everyone recognizes the kindness of the people, for whom living in harmony is a cultural fundamental element. Nobody doubts about their generosity in welcoming their fellow compatriots recently arrived, but no document mentions them. However, without their help, I do not see how we could have faced such an influx of refugees.

The French government gave strict instructions to the administration to accelerate and simplify the procedure of naturalization of the refugees. Where it used to take years to get a passport, the objective was

*to give it in 6 to 9 months. The official fig-
ures are difficult to interpret: some talk
about 200,000 immigrants, but there are
not only Vietnamese, but also Cambodians,
Laotians, Chinese... Most French people
do not know the difference.*

*Almost a thousand children are taken care
of by the welfare services and other charity, like the nuns. We all have at heart to
favour the blood relationship, trying to re-
unite families, find a parent, an uncle, an
aunt, a cousin... but the task is huge and
complicated. Although we aim for the same
goal, our methods and our resources are
different. It is surprising and sad to find
suspicion, even agressivity from some children welfare civil servants towards reli-
gious institutions.*

*However, I do not want to worry you with
issues, which, fortunately, do not have any
impact on you for now. Just be careful if*

you receive a visit from these services: tell Mother Superior right away.

I pray for you all and also for my godsons. When we find their family, I hope they will realize what you have done for them by allowing you to keep in touch with them. Who knows, maybe let you have them for the vacation, just as we do with grandparents?

In truth, I should tell you not to become too attached to them and not to have hopes up too high about the future, but I know it is not possible. I want to believe that if the Lord entrusted them to us, His purpose was for us all to be happy.

I can tell you right now that I will not be able to be with you for Christmas. Believe me, I regret it as much as you do, but you have to remember that I entered the Missionary Order to serve Jesus Christ through every little one He puts on my path. May He send you His divine grace. I give you kisses with all my love.

Sister Marie-Claire

LA FERME HAUTE, DECEMBER **1975**

My Dear Daughter,

It is a shame that you cannot be with us for Christmas. The snow has fallen, covering our mountains with a thick white blanket. You would have laughed, had you seen our little Pascal discover it for the first time. With Didier, they built a snowman much bigger than the little pitchoun. He has become so good and speaks better and better.

Benoît is starting to sit straight. He laughs out loud at this brother's funny faces. Pascal likes to stand in front of the mirror with his little brother. I think it comforts him to see how much they look alike. Go figure what is going on in their brains, but one thing is certain: those two boys are very close.

We took the kids to Carcassonne to see Santa Claus. Even the little one opened huge eyes at all the lights, the decoration and the toys. If I had listened to your brother, we should have bought the whole store. Finally, we agreed on a castle made of wooden blocks and knights for Pascal; some awakening toys with pretty colours and lots of noise for Benoît. Your brother asked us for a Polaroid... I told him it was way too expensive, but your father still bought him one. I believe he shares his son's wish to see right away the pictures we are going to take on Christmas when the kids open their gifts.

You are right when you say it is not possible not to love those two angels too much. I fear more than anything the day when you will announce to us that you have found their family. I'm trying to put my mind at rest by thinking, like you, that these people will become our friends and our Vietnamese family, that they will let us love our little treasures, because what's wrong with it?

Give us news from you. With all our love,

Your mother

CHARTRES, JANUARY **1976**

My dear family,

Mother Marie-Thérèse asked me to thank you for the parcel you sent, once more, mother, you are spoiling us. Remember that we made a vow of poverty. Fortunately, we are allowed on special occasions to celebrate around a meal and the whole community thanks you for your kindness.

It is a joy for me to know that my two protégés are doing well and that their happiness is shared with all of you. What a joy to see the pictures. They have grown so much, I sometimes wonder if they still remember me.

Heart's bonds

As for our inquiries, the situation is diffi-cult. There have been some acts of violence and many dead people. Information travels with difficulty from Vietnam, but thousands of people are still escaping any way they can.

We are working with the government by bringing our experience, our knowledge of the language and culture, so that help can take place. We are running up against pre-judice, difference and sometimes even hu-man stupidity.

We are torn apart between governmental directives insisting that the death of both parents must be proved to declare a child ready for adoption and hundreds of famil-ies ready to welcome little Vietnamese's children and offer them warmth, security and a normal life. Meanwhile, the children stay in an orphanage, where the love of nuns, employees and voluntary workers doesn't replace that of parents, where the lack of resources keeps them from being comfortable and well loved for the 'good of the children.'

The children in our institutions are better off, at least there is continuity in the nuns' services and we leave them when we can in foster homes care until at least one parent is found. As for the welfare services, the rule is to change foster home regularly to avoid too strong bounds between children and foster parents. Those are always paid to pretend it is just a job like any other. Such foolishness! My God, have those who write these laws never had a child? What kinds of blindness, of principles are guiding them on those dry lands where love and joy have no room? Who can think that a check every month will prevent people from loving each other? I do know that those who welcome little ones may need some financial help, without impeding the love they feel for the children, who are the reason they chose this path.

Heart's bonds

Every day, I thank the Lord to have allowed my godsons to be in your care. At least, they have a chance to grow in a healthy family environment just like every child should. Oh well, I am losing my temper again and if my mail was read, I would be in trouble. Take good care of my protégés. I love you. May God bless you.

Sister Marie-Claire

March 1976, La Ferme Haute

The nun is parking her car in the farmyard. Her heart is beating hard. While she was driving, one question did not stop haunting her: How will the children welcome her? What is left in their memories of the two months she spent comforting them, loving them with all her strength? The last six months, she has been trying to forget the intensity of the joy she felt as she was taking care of them. The disciplinary measures taken against her after her initiative did not seem like much to her. When she found herself at the bottom of the ladder again, doing the worst chores in the convent, she did it with great joy, without regretting one moment the decision she took last April 29th and 30th. Her smile and her radiance as she was doing lower tasks attracted so much admiration from the other sisters that she came back in the good grace of Mother Superior very quickly. However, humbly, Sister Marie-Claire could not see how she deserved it, since the happiness she knew thanks to the little boys could not be compared by any means with all the joy, although numerous, she had felt all these years as a novice and a then as missionary.

She steps down of her car and goes to the kitchen. Pascal is sitting next to Simone, both peeling potatoes, one with a peeler, the other one with a spoon.

-Hello, you are working hard, I see!
-Boudiou, here you are! You must have driven like crazy; we did not expect you so soon. We did not even hear the car.

Pascal seemed to be frozen for an instant, and then he throws his arms at her. Marie-Claire leans over him, the kid holds on to her neck. She stands up again, holding the boy in her arms.

-My darling, you recognize me!

The little one puts his head on her shoulder and squeezes harder.

-You are going to strangle me...

-Mommy, he says in Vietnamese.

Marie-Claire cannot hold her tears, her emotion so overwhelming. Unable to talk, she kisses the child.

-My little darling, I have missed you so much.

Simone, taken aback for a second, comes close to them and tries to take the little boy from her, but he does not let her. With all his strength, he holds on to the one who, in the confusion of his memories, is his mother.

When the first wave of joy has passed, the nun tries to put Pascal on the floor, but he will not let her either. With his arms and legs, all his strength is focusing on clinging to the one who, according to his heart, is his mom. Powerless because of his enthusiasm, Marie-Claire sits, with the child on her lap. Simone has given up the idea of separating them.

After a silence, she starts talking:
- I thought that everything was all right and that he would forget he was not born here, I do not know what to say or do anymore!
With a good timing, Benoît, who was sleeping, wakes up and starts calling. Simone goes to get him. The young woman tries to loosen the boy's grip, in vain. She is rocking the boy, stroking his back softly, singing a Vietnamese nursery rhyme.

Simone comes back with the little one, a little worried about how things will turn out.

-Come on now Pascal, let me hold Benoît in my arms.

The child releases a little his embrace but stays hung, opening one arm to welcome his little brother.

-A good thing I sat down, with this big baby and my little monkey, there is no way I could be standing up!

The baby smiles, babbling, pulling at his brother's hair then turns around to look for Simone. Relieved, she takes Benoît and puts him on her lap to feed him.

Fifteen minutes later, Louis and Didier arrive.

-What is going on? Asks Louis. We did not hear you talk, I thought nobody was there.

-Well, Pascal, you don't run at me to give me a kiss? Asks Didier, a little surprised by the serious atmosphere of the kitchen, usually full of noise and happiness.

Just like he did for Benoît, the child frees one arm to hold Didier, but keeps his three other limbs strongly around Marie-Claire, who he does not want to let go.

-He is hanging on to her like a stamp to a letter! Impossible to make him loosen his grip.
-Don't bother for that, life goes on; he will end up sleeping anyway. Let him tire himself away, says Louis, surprising everyone with his wisdom.

Somehow relieved by the sensible speech of her husband, Simone finds her composure again.
-You, my daughter, stay where you are. You Didier, set the table and you, Louis, go get us a bottle of nice wine in the basement...

All the afternoon long, Pascal did not release Marie-Claire. She persuaded him to take a bath, undresses him, washes him, dries him, helps him put on his pyjamas.

-Now, honey, you will walk like a big boy, I am tired of carrying you around, my back hurts.

-I sleep with you.

-If you are a good boy, but only tonight, promise, tomorrow you go sleep in your room.

-Yes, mommy.

The nun kneels so that her face is levelled with the one of the kid. She looks at him with all the love in the world.

-Listen sweetheart, I love you more than anything in the world; you know that, I can feel it. However, I am not your mommy; your mommy is Little Laughing Flower. She is also your brother's mommy. She gave birth to you. It is complicated but one day you will understand. Your mommy is in heaven and asked me to take care of you and your brother Benoît.

-Why did she go away?

-She could no longer live. You have seen flowers in a vase, one day they are beautiful and another one they lose all their colours.

-Did someone throw mommy in the garbage?

-No, she rests in a place called a cemetery. It is as if she was sleeping for a very very long time; but just like flowers sow other seeds to make other flowers, even prettier flowers, your mommy gave life to two wonderful boys. You cannot see her but she can see you.

-Just like when we play hide-and-seek with Didier?

-Pretty much, yes. When I was away from you, I thought of you very hard and I could see you in my heart. When I closed my eyes, I could see your eyes and your smile. I am your godmother.

-God Mother?

-A godmother is a second mommy; it is a big responsibility and a great joy. A godmother does not take a mommy's place, which is why I would like to teach you how to say a prayer in the evening, so that you can talk to her and keep her in your heart.

-With you.

-Yes, with me in your heart too.

The child holds Marie-Claire tight and she hugs him tenderly.

-We need to make room for Simone too, she is the one who takes care of you and loves you so much. She is a mother as well, your milk mother, it is complicated but you will understand one day. That is why she asks you to call her Mommy Simone. You have to promise me to stay nice with her.

-Yes, God Mother.

-Come now, they must be waiting for us for dinner.

Just like each time her daughter is visiting, Simone has prepared an excellent meal. Benoît seems to be the guest of honour in his high chair and looks happy with the festive atmosphere, the serious matters being postponed until tomorrow.

Heart's bonds

-I am going to bed like the hens tonight; I have had a long day full of emotion. Come, my little man, but do not forget our deal, one night only. Do you understand?
-Yes, God Mother.

Once kisses and hugs are given, the nun puts the child in her bed.
-Wait for me nicely; I am going to put on my nightgown.

While Marie-Claire is in the bathroom, the cat climbs next to Pascal, worried to see a change in her habits. She lets him stroke her, purrs but runs away as soon as the young woman comes back.
-You see, Pascal, even Samaou thinks that you should sleep in your own bed. Come now, I am going to teach you how to pray. You kneel at the foot of the bed, you hold your hands like this and you repeat after me: "Dear Mommy who is heaven, I love you with all my heart; help me be a good boy. Help me know and love Jesus. Amen."

-Who is Jesus?

-Our Lord, our Saviour, and the One I love and serve. Do not worry; you have all the time to get to know him.

Pascal needs to repeat the prayer a few times before he can say it by himself, but he tries with all his heart and good will. Once he has managed to do so, he puts his head on the pillow and falls right to sleep, smiling.

-Dear God, thank You for the happiness I receive with these children. Please may their love for me be no harm for them, may their happiness be greater than the sorrow of being seperated. Oh Holy Mary, Mother of God, mother of men, mother of all orphans, watch over my godsons, protect them...

Sister Marie-Claire spends most of the night praying, alternating thanks, demands, meditation and oraison. In the morning, exhausted, she carefully pushes Pascal who sleeps sideways and lying down next to him, sleeps hugging him tenderly.

The next day, Pascal is never far from Marie-Claire but he lets her take care of Benoît without showing any sign of jealousy. The young woman enjoys these moments of happiness, which she knows are counted. Benoît can now stand and try to walk. He needs constant attention, because he can walk very fast on all four, ready to discover the world, oblivious of the dangers.

-Mother, I admire you and your calm, you can do all your work smiling and the children are as happy as can be. They are so much more advanced than those in the orphanage are; and also a lot more joyful. They are happy here.
-When you called me last year, I was a little worried, I thought I was too old to take care of infants, well; it is the other way around, thanks to them I am ten years

younger! God knows how much I loved you and your brother, I had so much trouble getting pregnant, you were so desired, I never thought I would love anyone like I loved you and here I am head over heels about those two. And useless to talk about your father and brother! They are crazy about them, I cannot imagine what would happen if you find their family one day. I keep telling myself that we should wish for that, I just can't.

-That is exactly why the child welfare changes foster parents regularly. However, I cannot help thinking that the children best interest is stability surrounded by love.

-You said you had news, but since you have been here, I am still waiting for it.

-I am leaving for Vietnam. All the houses, which used to belong to the congregation, have been nationalized but they allow us to work in hospitals and dispensaries.

-When are you leaving? For how long?

-In a week and for three years. I do not know yet if I will have the chance to come back in-between, everything is so tense and confused there.

Slowly, tears stream down Simone's face. Her daughter takes her in her arms. Pascal looks up from the playpen where he is playing construction blocks with Benoît. He got off it, runs and throws himself on the women;
-Don't cry, I love you.

They hug the little boy, sniff and smile while crying. Feeling abandoned, the toddler starts crying too. Marie-Claire holds him.
-Don't cry, my little treasure, I love you too.
-You are going away again? Asks Pascal, worried.
-Yes, darling, I told you yesterday.
-For a long time?
-Yes, a long time.
-Then I go with you!

-That is not possible, you need to take care of Benoît, Didier, Mommy Simone and Daddy Louis.

-And Samaou, adds the child.

-You see, we need you here, but you stay in my heart.

Louis and Didier arrive then.

-What is wrong here, everybody is crying? Notices Louis.

-Your daughter is going back to Vietnam.

-We knew she would not stay for long in Chartres. However, honey, isn't that dangerous? They talk about atrocities carried out by the Khmers rouges.

-They are in Cambodia. It is not the same country. However, you are right; South Eastern Asia is going through a lot of troubles. We can be proud of our government and the help brought to refugees, both from charity organization and governmental agencies. Don't worry for me, my Order wouldn't send me back to Saigon, if I weren't expected there. For now, only hospitals and dispensaries are assigned to us. I will try to have the schools and orphanages reopen.

-How many sisters are going back? Asks Simone.

-For now, Sister Dao and myself. She is from North Vietnam and thinks that she can be useful. I can speak Vietnamese and I was the novice's mistress, so I know very well the sisters who stayed there last year when we escaped. I am very happy to see them again; we have so little news since mail is censored.

-Are you going to try to find information about the boys' family while you are there? Worries Didier.

-Yes, of course, I should.

A heavy silence sets in, the joy of yesterday all of a sudden gone.

MAY 1976, HO CHI MINH VILLE

My dear family,

I am sorry I did not write to you sooner, but my return to Saigon was a bit difficult. The name of the city has changed, as you know, but also its aspect. Such a shame! The war has damaged everything and the rest of the buildings, which were bombed, have not been cleaned; this feels like war, especially with the omnipresence of soldiers. We have not been able to get the school buildings back, so I am still at the hospital, where unfortunately, we need everything. We must keep a low profile. We hear about former civil servants, South-Vietnamese soldiers, prisoners, but also all those suspected to have occidental friends, sent by thousands to 're-education' camps.

Heart's bonds

You remember World War II; you may imagine what is going on here. I have no idea if my mail will go through you because censorship is quite strict. There is also a massive exodus: in just a year, hundreds of thousand people left the city. With so little information about the kids' family, it seems even more complicated to look among refugees here than in France. Distress is everywhere and few people have enough to eat.

As for the reopening of the school and the orphanage, it seems much compromised for now. I will probably stay a few more months with the sisters at the hospital where I am most needed here as a practical nurse. I am in no danger whatsoever, you can be sure.

I was very happy to see the sisters who used to be novices, for whom I am now responsible, and our community is strong and radiant in spite of the difficulties we are facing.

Most important of all, give a big kiss to my little boys from me, and keep my sisters and myself in your prayers, we need them.

Be sure that I keep you in my prayers and my deep tenderness. God bless you.

Sister Marie-Claire

Heart's bonds

SEPTEMBER 1976, La Ferme Haute

My dear daughter,

It took over two months to your letter to arrive. It was high season here and I had no time to answer. You can easily imagine how worried I am to know you are so far away from us, living in precarious conditions such as you described.

You signed up as a missionary to take care of children and here you are, emptying pots! Can't you ask to go to another country and teach there? You talk about a few months, but as long as you do not have a safe position that corresponds to your studies and your wish, I cannot imagine how you could be happy. I am sorry but I cannot help finding it unfair.

Well, enough with the whining... Here, everything is fine. We have had a very successful season; every room was continually full and we even had to serve dinner and lunch seven days a week. Fortunately, we were able to hire a few young kids from the village, which made everyone happy.

As you can imagine, Pascal cried a few nights after you left, then he seemed to accept it. He kisses your picture every night before going to bed. The two pitchouns are doing well. They are starting to grow. Although they are still smaller than the local children are their age, they have cheeks are becoming more full, which is a relief for me.

Do you remember little Isabelle, the daughter of the innkeeper? Well, she is a schoolteacher and was assigned in Saissac to teach in pre-school. Since she comes here regularly to go horse riding, she has grown fond of your godsons and encouraged me to enrol Pascal for the school start this year. I did not agree. I would rather keep him here at least one more year before letting him go among kids who could push him around. So Isabelle offered to come on Wednesdays to take care of him and give him activities to do just like at school; in return she can go horse riding on Sundays. I did not really need her to teach the pitchoun to draw, colour and these kinds of things, but she is so nice that I could not say no.

Didier entered sixth grade this year, he needs to take the bus early in the morning to go to Revel. He is going to have very long days and will not have so much time for the little boys anymore. Fortunately, Benoît can walk now and the two brothers play increasingly together.

Heart's bonds

Your father has taken to convert the attic into a large room for Didier. Since he is going to be in middle school, your brother wants to have a desk in his bedroom rather than do his homework on the kitchen table as he used to. As a result, we gave his room to the two little boys and Didier sleeps in your room while the work is not finished. It is not too hard to put the boys in bed but the nights are quite restless: either Benoît wakes up and comes to find comfort between your father and me, while Pascal goes to Didier's bed, or the other way around... They will eventually have to stop wandering like that at night before your brother has a room upstairs, but I have to say that when the little pitchoun snuggles up to me, I don't have the heart to put him back into bed. Ah, Benoît, probably because I carried him around all the time for months, it seems that he is one of my own. And in return, he is such a great hugger! Pascal is more independent, plus he's always following the men, but Benoît, peuchère, he is every mother's dream. Do not be jealous, but neither you nor your brother were attached to me like that. I do not know if it is due to his young age or the circumstance, but what is for sure is that I, too, am starting to become crazy about him.

That is about it on our side, your father and I are doing well. Here, life goes on. The days are starting to be seriously shorter and its autumn blanket covers the Black Mountain, the mushrooms are everywhere and I think of you who like them so much in an omelette. I will dry some and send them to you.

Everybody says hello and we hope to see you soon.

Your mother

NOVEMBER 1976, HO CHI MINH

My dear family,

Thank you for your long letter and all the good news, which help me, imagine your life right now.
Here, nothing has changed, do not worry about me, I am very happy to serve where I am most needed, and unfortunately, there are a lot of people in need here. No nurse certification is necessary here before one can start giving care and I am learning every day.

It feels good to be among my sisters, I am not planning to ask for any change. I am still hoping that one day we will be able to reopen schools and orphanages and I wish with all my heart to be a part of it.

I think of you all, try to send me recent pictures of the kids, at that age, they must be changing so fast! I know you and I know you do not want me to thank you for everything you are doing for them but I want you to know that it brings me such a joy.

I send you kisses. Keep my Sisters and me in your prayers. May God's grace be upon you.

Love,

Sister Marie-Claire

DECEMBER 1976, LA FERME HAUTE

My dear daughter,

Time is going by so fast. This is already the second Christmas with your protégés, and I remember like yesterday when you arrived with them.

Benoît gave us a big scare. Poor little boy was very ill and your father and I took turns for three days to be with him, so that he would not be alone. He had such a dysentery that we could not even put on diapers. You cannot imagine how worried I was. Fortunately, all of his exams came back with nothing serious and four teeth came out all at once: that is what bothered him! He lost almost two pounds, Doctor Lerasle told me that it is nothing, that he will gain them back quickly, but peuchère, he looks so pale. The whole family was worried. We even lit candles to la Madonna! Thank God, everything is all right now.

Father Benoît spent a few days with us after Christmas, he wanted to take care of his godsons, since their godmother is so far away. At first, your father and I were a little intimidated, but he quickly put us at ease. He is a remarkable man, but I kept an eye on him, I do not want him to brainwash Didier about becoming a priest, I gave my daughter to God, that should be enough without him taking my boy too!

Here are some pictures, as you can see, we were happy that day; you were the only one missing. Once again, do not be worried about seeing Benoît a little thin, he is get-

ting back in shape faster than I am recovering from my fear.

We send you kisses and look forward to having some news.

Your mother

Heart's bonds

APRIL 1977, LA FERME HAUTE

My beloved daughter,

Your letters are quite rare and very short. You do not tell us much about what is going on, which is no relief for me. I have no doubt that if you had any good news; you would hurry to tell us, which is why I am worried. I am glad that your parcel for Christmas arrived, even if it took two months.

Here, low season has already started. We had guests during spring break and every weekend is full until the summer.

On top of chocolate bunnies for Easter, Pascal had quite an unusual gift: can you imagine, Samaou, his cat, gave birth to her kittens on his bed! I had never seen such a thing, usually cats hide their babies but this one is not stupid and knew that the pitchoun would protect her little ones. Fortunately, there are only four, but this time I need to take her to the vet and have her neutered, otherwise we are going to have a breeding stock. You would think your father would have shown authority? Well, it only made him laugh! When I think of how hard he was with you, his daughter, his princess, as he said, and here he is, yielding to a little boy.

Didier received a special award for his grades, can you imagine! I was worried to see him go to middle school, with all the changes in our lives. Well, he has never worked so hard. He too, grows too fast, if you do not hurry to come back, he will have hair on his chin when you see him again.

Heart's bonds

As you can see on our side, we only have good news. Of course, I will not bother you with our stories of the barn roof falling out or the difficulty we have with a mare to give birth, only minor daily trouble for an activity like ours.

We all hope to see you soon. Everybody gives you lots of hugs and kisses.

Your mother

JULY 1977, VIETNAM

My dear family,

We need your prayers and thoughts. I left Ho Chi Minh to reach the countryside in the South, where we have a dispensary, which is not approved yet but with very few resources. Sister Anh and Sister Dao came with me. You know how much I love them and thanks to them, even the hardest days are full of joy. Without waiting for a special authorization, we decided to welcome abandoned children. Most of them are met-is, their mothers fearing reprisals for complicity with the enemy." Dear God, men are so predictable in their injustice! Whether we are in Asia or in Europe, it is always for the innocent people to pay for their parents breaches. Many soldiers had family back home, but the poor girls believed in the reality of their union. But they went they left, the majority of them abandon women and children. Because of the war, misery, and fear, the mothers give their children to our care and try to reach their village and find support among their family. Some of them stay close enough to come and see their children regularly and bring some help, but most disappear without a trace. At least here, we have a little bit of land for farming, which allows us to grow vegetables and feed a dozen hens which give us eggs. Although they are extremely poor, the peasants bring us rice, sometimes old clothes, which we can transform to fit the kids. The help sent by our motherhouse and donators do not always arrive here.

Here is my advice for the parcels you send us: make small ones, minimize the content and only send what is necessary. I thank you for everything you do for us here and for my dear godsons with you. May the Lord Jesus bring you grace for all you do. Know that the five of you are in our daily prayers. I send you a lot of hugs and kisses.

Sister Marie-Claire

Heart's bonds

SEPTEMBER 1977, LA FERME HAUTE

-Boudiou, you are so handsome! Says Simone, looking at Pascal, dressed with new clothes and shoes with his first school bag on his back.

The child is beaming with pride. A hundred times, he took out and then put back all his school supplies: a large box of crayons, colouring pencils, little scissors with a round tip, glue, paper, pencil box with a nice pencil sharpener in a shape of the earth, a white eraser, and a few black pencils. Such a treasure! In addition, the little metal box with a beautiful drawing of a fire truck containing his snack: an apple, a slice of cake, a milk chocolate bar with hazelnuts and a little jar with apple juice.

Pascal has been dreaming about going to pre-school for so long, that he can barely believe that the day has finally come. He is the hero of the day. The whole family takes him to school.

-Most of all, at school, you must call Isabelle "Miss Isabelle". And do not forget to give your tickets for the cafeteria. Do not eat your snack before this afternoon recess. You do not go out of school; you wait for me to pick you up...

Simone showers him with advices.

-Stop now, you're going to give him a headache with all your talking! Interrupts Louis.

-We are leaving this poor little boy among savages and you don't find anything else to say?

-You are exaggerating; they are only the village kids.

-Don't worry, Pascal, says Didier. I made many friends at school; I even remember a few fights with fondness.

-My God, I hope that the boy will be less naughty than you were.

-What are you talking about: if every child were as naughty as our Didier was, the world would be better.

-You will tell me everything, my boy, right.

-For once, he is a boy, not a sissy; goes on Louis; he will not be a sneak, he will learn how to defend himself, it never hurt anyone.

-Mom, Dad, you are taking him to school, not to a detention camp. There is no reason to panic; you will end up scaring him.

-I am not even scared, answers Pascal with a large smile on his face.

-Park the car here, we cannot get any closer, says Simone to Louis.

-Alright, I am taking him to the schoolyard and then I take my bus, you do not need to step out of the car, says Didier while opening the door.

Simone goes out of the car:

-I am going too, if he cries too much, I am taking him back home.

Once at the school door, Pascal sees Isabelle. After a quick kiss given to Simone, he runs to the teacher, without even turning back. Happy to see that the first school day starts well, Didier turns to his mother.

-But, why are you crying? Everything is going to be all right! He says with surprise.

-They are all the same, all ungrateful! Ah, we hug you, comfort you, spoil you, but you only think about going and leaving us. Your sister and you both did the same to me, I worry, but you do not care about that! In addition, you are leaving to Revel, oh God, why are they growing so fast?

Relieved that his mother is only crying because of a heart too full of love, he gives her a kiss and runs to take his bus.

The first weeks of school are eventless, until one evening, before dinner, Simone notices that Pascal is not playing with his brother as he usually does. Because of the rain and the cold, he is not allowed to play outside, as for the working area in the attic, Simone forbids him to go there, because of all the nails, the hammers and other tools which she thinks are dangerous in his hands.

-Pascal, where are you? It is not the time to play hide and seek, you know that I need to prepare dinner.

Hearing no answer, she goes to search him and finds him in the bathroom, cutting his hair.

-I can't believe it! Why are you doing such a silly thing?

There are locks of hair here and there, wherever the boy was able to find hair with his pair of scissors.

-It is a complete mess you have done here, are you crazy or what?

-I don't have pretty hair! And I look like a girl.

-Not pretty, your hair? Mother of God, can You hear that one? Your hair is gorgeous:

black, thick, easy to comb... and what that
story about looking like a girl? Who could
put such silly ideas in your head?

-No, look at you, Daddy Louis and Didier,
you have wavy hair, soft and fine...

-But sweetheart, yours are much prettier
than ours are!

-No, and have you seen my eyes? They are
black and small and yours are large and
brown...

The child starts to cry softly and goes on:
even my skin is different...

-What is this nonsense? Who told you such
foolishness? It is true that we are not completely alike, but look, we are the same:
two eyes, two ears, one nose, one mouth,
two arms, two legs... That is all that matters... If everyone was the same, how could
we recognize one from another? Some are
tall or small, thin or fat, why does it matter?

-But I am a dirty chink and I look like a
girl!

-Tell me who told you such a monstrosity and I will cut him in small pieces and make up sausages with his guts! What a shame, Good Mother, it is not possible to hear such abominations!

-I'm not a sneak. But a lot of them tell me that I am one.

-What about the teacher? She doesn't say anything?

-It is in the schoolyard, she cannot hear.

-Well, she is going to hear me, and very soon.

-No, please, they will say again that I am the teacher's pet and it will be worse.

-Well, pre-school is not mandatory, you are not going back.

-Please, I want to go to school.

Didier comes close and interrupts:

-I heard everything. Well, calm down. First, we ask Dad to cut his hair real short to repair the damage, we have dinner and we talk about what we should do. I cannot beat up little kids but I can scare them.

-And Mister Didier is giving orders to his mother now?

-Of course not, Mom, I am just trying to help things out.

-You mean that when little brats call the boy dirty chink, you only want to 'help things out'?

-What is wrong? The table is not set, says Louis, surprised when he steps in too. What is that meeting in the bathroom all about?

Once updated, Louis took things in his hands.

-My boy, first, the next time somebody calls you a chink, you answer: "I'm Vietnamese and proud to be", that will close his mouth. He will not know what to say to that. In life, you will never be able to please everyone; there are mean people, stupid people, but most of all many ignorant people. Your godmother bought you a book about Vietnam, you are going to take it to school and you are going to explain that your country is a beautiful country, that

France is a friend of your country and that people there are different but just as smart as the smartest Frenchmen are. That there is neither shame nor glory to be born in a country or another, that is only luck, what matters is the qualities of the heart and nobody has the monopole with that.

-What is 'nono Paul'?

-It means that everyone can choose to be nice, helpful, and brave. You see, you will show them that you are not afraid of them, that their nastiness does not affect you anymore. Whom are you going to believe? Little brats who are jealous of you or your family, here, who loves you? If we tell you that, you are perfect the way you are, that it is not important if we are different and that we love you as much as parents can love their child, who are you going to believe?

-Papa Louis, I love you. Pascal throws himself into his arms and holds him tight against his heart.

-Good, Didier you set the table, Simone, you prepare dinner, I take care of pitchoun and we forget what happened.

-Well, I certainly will not forget! Retorts Simone, going back to the kitchen. On her way, she grabs Benoît who is still playing nicely with his blocks, without being troubled by the crying and the screaming. She holds him tight and kisses him.

-If anybody hurts you, there will be a crime in Saissac!

Of course, Simone cannot help going to Isabelle to tell her what happened, mentioning Pascal's fear about a possible retaliation. Tactful, the teacher prepares a small presentation about the seven continents for the pupils and takes advantage of it to talk about differences, insisting on the notion of equality and fraternity, cherished by the French republic. The children cut out little people of different colours, holding hands and forming a circle around the globe.

Heart's bonds

A few days later, Pascal leaves school happy.

-Mommy Simone, I have a new friend. He has just arrived. His name is Yannick. He told me that if someone bothers me, he would give him a punch in the nose.

-Are there still people bothering you? Worries Simone.

-No, just in case...

-You know that fighting is no good, is your Yannick fighting often?

-No, but he is the tallest in the class and his father is a police officer!

-Are you sure it isn't something he says just to be important?

-No, it is true, he even has a gun.

-I will see with Isabelle. If that little boy is respectable, I will invite him next Wednesday at the farm.

-What is 'respectable'?

-That you can invite him home without having me worried that you will do silly things.

-I promise, Mommy Simone, we will not do any silly thing.

Heart's bonds

OCTOBER 1977, LA FERME HAUTE

My dear daughter,

It took two months for you letter to arrive, again. Are you sure that you are in no danger of ending up in jail, or worse. Obviously, it is useless to ask you to go to a more peaceful place. You have always been so stubborn and done the opposite of what we told you to do. I bet that your vow of obedience is harder to respect that the vow of poverty, in spite of the misery you are describing us. Compared to that, our little troubles seem very small.

Pascal goes to pre-school. He made a very good friend, Yannick. His father is from Martinique, he is a police officer. His mother is from Brittany, which makes a very handsome mix. They have been here for dinner a few times at the host restaurant and we have become friends. They come from an island, where it is always warm. Poor souls, they are going to have a hard time going through winter in our climate!

Didier teaches Yannick how to ride on a pony. Pascal is already quite a good rider, even though he is young and small. As for Benoît, he asks for a turn and always gives us a great smile when Didier takes him in front of him.

Here are pictures of us all. We miss you. Is it asking too much to hope having you over for Christmas? We send you lots of kisses. Here are a few drawings from Pascal for his 'God Mother' and 'sketches' from Benoît who wants to be part of it.

With much love,
Your mom.

Heart's bonds

Excitement is at a peak on that beautiful morning of may. Marie-Claire was granted a few days off to come for Pascal's first Communion. It is the first time in four years that she is coming back to France. She is accompanied by the Monseigneur Benoît, the boys' godfather, recently named bishop. Of course, all of Saissac is aware of this great news, since the priest announced during church that two bishops were coming, the one of Carcassonne coming for the occasion. This has never been seen in this little town.

The family and friends will be celebrating, among them, Yannick's family; those coming from Brittany and La Martinique booked rooms in La Ferme Haute.

-Here they are, here they are! Shout the boys who went scouting on the high rock to watch the road.

Since they met three years ago, Pascal and Yannick have never been apart. They share the same passion for poneys, cats (Pascal offered one of Samaou's kitten to Yannick) and their studies. They have become used to doing their homework together, challenging each other to be the best. Obviously, Benoît follows them around and holds on to them as much as he can, walking on the top of his foot to show that he is 'almost as big as his brother.'

Although they rarely see their godfather and have not seen their godmother for years, the boys love them very much, the connection is kept alive thanks to mail, rare phone calls but also pictures and discussion with Simone, Louis and Didier who feed the memories and feeling of the children.

As she hears the boys scream, Simone take her apron off, puts her hair in place, takes a look of herself in the mirror in an attempt to be relieved that she still looks good and runs in toward the farm yard to welcome the newcomers.

-Louis, come quick, you will say hello to Monseigneur while I kiss our daughter.

This was without counting on the boys' swiftness, who jumped on the car doors as soon as it stopped. Their godfather becoming a bishop does not keep them from jumping to his neck. Yannick stayed a little behind, waiting for the end of the excitement to come forward.

Marie-Claire enjoys their open signs of affection and holds the boys in her arm very tight.

-What about me? I count for nothing now? Simone shouts out, faking to be angry.

-Mom!

-Let me look a you. Hey, you'll soon be able to walk behind a poster without ungluing it, it isn't possible to be that thin! Tell me, My Lordship, have you seen the skinny cat coming back from over there!

-Come one Simone, you're not going to call me 'My Lordship'! Have you forgotten my name?

-Of course not, but now I won't be able to call you Benoît anymore, and anyway, there is only one Benoît for me and that is the little one.

-Come on in, come into the house, interrupts Louis. You're just on time for the appetizer and the bottle of Limoux is just cold enough.

-Pascal, will you introduce me to your friend Yannick, don't let him look at us alone. Come here, don't be shy.

Didier arrives and runs to kiss his sister.

-Well, am I dreaming or what? You're scratching my cheek and you're taller than me!

-That's normal, I'm a man now!

-At fifteen?

-Sixteen in two months and eighteen soon!

-That's a way to see it.

Both brother and sister start laughing, which makes the little ones laugh too.

A wind of happiness blows on La Ferme Haute.

The meal is joyful, each one has a thousand things to tell about the last few years. Everyone listens to Sister Marie-Claire with attention, as she talks about her difficulties, but also her victory:

-The sisters are going to be able to reopen one school. It's only a beginning, but it is a great hope. Life is always difficult in Vietnam, but the toughest years are behind us. There are still a lot of abandoned children. We don't see new metis but very poor children, whose parents cannot feed them any-more. A majority of girls, because in these countries, boys are considered as a poten-tial support for the family, while girls are seen as a burden. There is still a lot to do. Most important is to get authorization for the occidentals to adopt. The difficulty stems from the fact that visas are refused and that a Mafia network is in place, trying to sell the children. We are lucky to be in a large city. Isn't it sad that politics keeps hu-manitarians cause from working properly? People disagree about adoption by foreign-ers but when I see my two godsons beam-ing of joy, it confirms that what a child needs most is love and security. Of course, it would be best if they could stay in their country and their culture, but when that is not possible to find a family for them, then yes, we should do everything to give them a real home, whatever the origin may be... oh, I feel ashamed; I'm the only one talk-ing...

-Your heart is overwhelmed, Marie-Claire, it is good for you to talk. We need your enthusiasm and your conviction to go on. Louis, Simone, the Lord blessed you a daughter like yours!

-Believe me, it isn't easy for a mother to have her child on the other side of the world, to know that she doesn't eat enough every day, to fear that something might happen to her... Without the two little treasures she brought us, I think I may have been angry at Him, the Lord, to have taken her away from me.

-Careful, Simone, you're talking to a bishop! worries Louis.

-Before everything else, I'm a friend and a brother in Christ. Don't be afraid to tell me your feelings. How many great prophets and great saints have complained to God about their lot ?

While the adults talked, Didier and the children go to the stable, saddle the ponies and go on a ride.

After coffee, Louis, Simone and Marie-Claire prepare the next day festivities, while Bishop Benoît goes down to Saissac to talk about the service with the priest.

At dinner, the conversation is mainly about the big day. The weather forecast a sky with no cloud and a temperature above normal for the season: everything should go well.

When it is time to go to bed, sister Marie-Claire wonders whether one of the kids will ask to sleep with her, but after giving a kiss to everybody, both go nicely into their room. The nun has a moment of nostalgia as she remembers Pascal hung to her a few years back. She feels a tear drop at the corner of her eyes and starts thinking about all the children in the orphanage, the room with too many beds in it, the babies in hammocks... She smiles, thinking about all those little ones who need her so much. She must not regret her choice, but again, she can feel what it cost her. She kneels in her room and spends most of the night praying.

The bells are calling out, cars are parking everywhere, but the police officers, nicely, only make sure that the roads are not blocked and leave people park partially on the pavement. Party is in the air. The children dressed in white, the little girls hair braided with fresh flowers look so serious that everyone, believer or not, is moved and remember when he or she was 8 and pure.

The church is decorated with flowers, the beautiful songs can be heard from outside, the doors staying open since not every one is able to enter.

The children come forward for their first Communion. Simone and Louis cannot keep from crying of pride and joy, as Pascal receives the Host from his godfather. His heart is full of joy. He has never been so happy, he feels complete, around those he loves. He will never forget this blissful feeling. He has a thought for his 'mother in heaven.' He is certain that Little Laughing Flower is looking at him proudly. He has no memory of her. In his mind, she is 'one' with his godmother.

After all, for a child, living in Heaven or on the other side of the world is about the same thing, although he is being told that one needs nothing because she is with God and the other one gives everything for Him. Strange trade and not easy to understand, but what matters today is that Marie-Claire is here, just for him. He cherishes this thought. He remembers feeling like 'the ugly duckling when the other children called him 'chink'; it all seems so far away now. He looks for Yannick and smiles at him. This morning, almost the whole class is having first Communion and the children feel mysteriously close. They have been taught that they are all brothers and sisters, yes, but Benoît is more a brother than the others, thinks Pascal. Lost in his thoughts, he has not realized that the service is over. His friend gives him a slight punch on the side, they try not to laugh out loud and go up the aisle.

After the ceremony, as the children are leaving first, the cameras click everywhere. Lined up in size, Pascal is the first and Yannick the last, all the children are beaming with joy and pride. The priest and both bishops arrive outside the church and behind them is a cheerful bustle with kisses, calling one another, cars hunking to attract attention of some passenger.

It takes some time to gather all the guests and reach La Ferme Haute; some temporary tables were assembled and covered with white napkins and flowers in the farmyard. Quite a few people are working hard to finish preparing. When she arrives, Simone hurries in the kitchen to supervise. Foie gras, duck filet with boletus, potatoes with black truffles, salad, cheese and the unavoidable pièce montée* will be the menu for the day.

-Please Godmother, will you come too for my Communion? asks Benoît.
-My darling, I wish it with all my heart, but unfortunately, I cannot promise you anything, my life doesn't belong to me. It is already a great chance to have been able to come today.
-You like Pascal best?
-No, my love. I love you both just as much. Come on my knees.

Marie-Claire kisses him and holds him against her heart.
-I hope we will both be there for you, my boy. I will pray for it and you too, from now on, alright? asks the bishop.
-Of course, godfather!

*A traditional decorative confectionery centrepiece in a sculptural form used for formal banquets

Heart's bonds

A large smile lights up the little boy's face, who relieved, jumps on the floor and runs to follow his brother and his friend.

The day goes by like a dream. Everything is perfect, some days stay engraved forever in the hearts as moments of grace; we forget everything that is not part of this special instant and have a taste of eternity, before it vanishes in the past.

The same night, the bishop Benoît takes the road again, taking with him Sister Marie-Claire.

EASTER 1982, LA FERME HAUTE

It is still cold on this day, April 11, 1982. The spring sun has difficulty fighting against humidity and the clouds keep hiding the sky, however, early that day, on Easter morning, the whole house is excited. Everyone is expecting the coming birth of a little foal, even more than the chocolate eggs. Of course, it is not the first time that a mare is giving birth, but this time, something very important is at stake: if it is a female, she will be given to Pascal, a male being too difficult to master for a young boy of 10. Since they never knew the exact birth date of the boy, Easter Day, which changes every year, was chosen as his birthday and it is this day that Didier's mare is about to conceive. Such a coincidence cannot be just a chance and the children hope with their all hearts that Pascal's prayer will be granted.

Although labour has started early morning, time for church has come and Simone has great difficulties taking the boys there, Didier and Louis staying by the mare.

'Dear God, may it be a female, dear God, may it be a female...' Both kids cannot manage to follow the service and to keep their thoughts away from the mare. The service is barely over that they drag Simone, without giving her time to talk with her friends, neighbours, clients, nor even greeting the priest. When they arrive at the farm, they jump out of the car and run to the horse pen. The vet is there. Louis called him for help, the mare showing signs of great difficulties. Finally, the little one comes out just when the children arrive. The foal seems to be very dark, lying with his mother licking it with care. Everybody is waiting. The mare pushes it with her nose, after two or three unsuccessful trials, the little one manages to stand on its frail legs, trembling. The mare keeps licking and encouraging him. From where they are, the children cannot see whether it is a male or a female. None of the three men makes any comment and it wrings Pascal's heart. The mare keeps encouraging her foal, who manages two or three clumsy steps. Its coat is black, a pretty white star is on its forehead. Finally, Louis breaks the silence after a few minutes which seemed like hours to the boys.

-So Pascal, how are you going to call your foal?

Elated, the boy starts crying.
-Why are you crying, didn't you want a girl? says Benoît, surprised.
-It's just that I am so happy!
Didier walks to him and carries him to the foal.

-Now, you are responsible of her. Do you promise to always take good care of her?
-I promise, you will teach me and I will be as good a master as you are.

He sets a hand on the trembling animal.
-Nice girl, it's me.
-So, have you thought of a name yet, asks Louis?
-I'm going to call her Shooting Star.
-That's a good choice, my boy, comments Louis.

The rain is starting to fall, but everyone stays here, once more amazed by the miracle of life, united and happy. A lightning and thunder break that magical moment.
Louis ask the vet:
- Paul, come on for a drink to cheer with us before you go.
-Can we stay at the stable? ask Pascal.
-No, they need calm. Come, you will have long years to enjoy her, now, let's celebrate Easter.

The telephone rings. Bishop Benoit never forgets to call his godsons on this day. His phone calls and his letters are always a great joy for the boys. Pascal tells him every detail about the birth of his foal, Benoît become impatient and almost tears the handset off from his brother.

-When are you coming to see us, godfather?

-Next month, my boy. I want to congratulate you on your good results in Kindergarten, Simone tells me you recieved a prize. I hope you are just as good in catechism.

-I'm the best!

-Very good. And can you read now?

-Yes, very well, I even read some of Pascal's books.

-Good, excellent, I will bring you both a few beautiful stories about the Saints. Now, can I talk to Simone, please?

Regretfully, the child gives her the phone.

-Happy Easter, My Lordship, it is so nice of you not to forget us.

-How could I? I'm in charge of souls, answers the bishop laughing. I need to talk to you and Louis about the boys. Do you happen to have three available rooms in the beginning of June, after Pentacost?

-For you, there is always room. You say three, will Christine be with you?

-Sister Marie-Claire cannot come back right now; I will be with my chauffeur and my secretary.

-Is there a problem with the boys?

-Not at all, just some administrative paperwork. Don't you worry, everything is alright. It is just that I'd rather come and explain than do everything by phone.

-You could write, Pentacost is far away!

-50 days but no reason to worry. Well, happy Easter to you all and see you very soon.

He hungs up.

-I only heard half of the conversation, says Louis, what is going on?

-His Lordship is coming to see us in June. We'll talk about it later, there's still plenty to do, the doctor has to go home soon and it is time we had lunch.

-We didn't look for the eggs!

-Don't you worry, my dear Benoît, they will still be here after lunch, go and try to do justice to my lamb rost and you will have the whole afternoon to find them.

-When I am as big as Pascal, will I have a foal too ?

-I promise, but you need to eat meat and vegetables if you want to be big enough one day to ride a horse, otherwise you will spend your life on a pony.

-When will I have my own pony?

-It's a secret, answers Didier.

-Come on, we won't keep the pitchoun in suspense, not today! Says Simone, always ultra protective of her 'little one.'

-It was supposed to be a surprise, but alright, it's a shame for you though, you're going to be impatient, adds Louis, making the suspense last a little longer.

-Tell us, when? Say the brothers together.

-For your seventh birthday, Didier answers smiling.

-But that is very soon! Benoît is beaming of joy. Can I choose him?

-You're very demanding now, my boy, says Louis smiling.

-Since it isn't a surprise anymore, we should leave him the pleasure of choosing, interrupts Simone.

-I know already, I want Prince, I've always dreamt about it. He's my favourite and it always make me angry when somebody else is riding him and doesn't treat him right. I don't like those who don't know how to take care of ponies or horses and who pull too hard on the bit or kick them. When I'm big, I will be a vet, just like Docteur Paul, and if someone hurts animals, I will put them in jail.

-Police officer put people in jail, not vets, rectifies Pascal laughing.

-Well, then I will be a vet police officer, answers Benoît, proudly.

-You're right, my boy, and you, big boys, don't laugh at him like silly, don't worry, honey, you are so smart you can easily invent a new job if you want.

-Simone always wants to have the last word, that's the privilege of mothers, but let's get back to our ponies. Prince is brave, but he's already ten, wouldn't you prefer a younger pony, who you could train and with whom you could do competition? asks Louis, surprised by the choice.

-I love Prince.

-I told you, steps in Didier. I know my little brother and I know how he loves that pony.

-Well, if he is THE ONE you want, he's the one you get, concludes Simone.

-For real? Nobody else but me will ride him?

-Yes, but you will have to take care of him every day, warns Louis.

-It's the best day of my life! Can I call godfather to tell him right away?

-No, don't bother him, but you can send him a card, now that you know how to write.

-And also, one to Godmother.

-We are both going to write to her then, I will help you and we will send pictures of Shooting Star and Prince.

-That's a great idea, Simone smiles, enjoying the children's happiness.

-And don't forget the egg hunt.

-Yes, Didier, come with us.

After the three boys left, Simone turns to Louis:

-I didn't know such happiness was possible. If anyone took them away from me now, I think I would die.

-Don't be silly, Simone, come now, lets' take a nap.

Louis puts tenderly his arm around his wife's shoulder. He does not show his affection much, neither talk about it, but the light on his look drives away the little cloud which darkened his wife's eyes.

JUNE 1982, LA FERME HAUTE

The bishop's sedan stops in front of Saissac school. Bishop Benoît told Simone, that he would be just on time to pick up the children after school. When the boys see their godfather at the door, they leave their classroom line to run towards him. Fortunately, the bishop is very well known since Pascal's Communion and nobody is offended that they breach the rule. The boys have barely time to give a kiss to their godfather before a whole crowd gathers around them, each one trying to greet the important man.

Pascal and Benoît hold him tight, both proud and jealous of the time he spends with the others, young or adults, saying a nice word or giving a blessing. When they arrive at La Ferme Haute, they drag their godfather and his acolytes to the stables, without giving them time to take care of their luggage. Simone, who saw the car coming, runs outside.

-My Lordship, what are you going to think about us with those pitchouns who take you without giving you time to have a glass of water!

-Don't you worry, Simone, I think I have two very happy godsons and I am de-lighted. Remember the words of Jesus Christ: 'Let the little children come to me', you have no idea how nice it is to be with them.

-But not in a stable!

-Why not? Horses and ponies are beautiful and they also are God's creatures. You really spoiled the children, I would have loved to have a pretty horse like Shooting Star when I was a boy.

-And not a pony like Prince? asks Benoît, always worried that his older brother might be the favourite one.

-Yes, and also a beautiful pony like Prince. But Simone is right, I would like a glass of water. You know Father Emmanuel already and this is Father Bonafieu.

-Nice to meet you, Father. Come let's go into the house.

For the first time, the air is tight in the house, Simone and Louis are impatient for the children to go to bed, whereas the children are used to stay up late when their godfather is here, and are in no rush. The bishop takes them to their room to put them to sleep. At the table, the adults and Didier wait for him to come back to talk about the reason for his visit.

-I am sorry I had you waiting, but I prefer talking to you first before we talk to the kids. It's been already seven years since the Saigon drama. We have been looking for the children's father, both in France and in Vietnam, without finding him. According to the French law, a missing person is considered dead after seven years. The children are now considered as orphans, thus ready for adoption.

-Do you mean that we could now adopt the pitchouns and that nobody could ever take them from us?

-In the best cases, yes. If I asked Father Bonafieu to come with me, it is because he is also a lawyer; he is going to explain to you the different options and steps that need to be done. The first question you need to answer is whether you wish a simple adoption or a full one.

-What does it mean? ask both Simone and Louis.

-In the first case, the children have a status of 'adopted', in the second one, they are your legitimate children.

-Can you explain, Father?

-If you choose the full adoption, Pascal and Benoît will appear in your family records certificate, just like if they were born from you. They will have exactly the same rights as your legitimate children, for example on your will, which is why you need the authorization of your children. Didier is going to be eighteen, I believe.

-I don't need to wait for my birthday to say that I agree. To me, they are already my brothers, I will be happy to share with them everything.

-You spontaneity honours you, Didier, I knew you would react like this, just like I vouch for Marie-Claire that she won't hesitate a second.

-There's no problem, then!

-For you and for us, no, but the administration doesn't see things so easily. There are unfortunately so many families that tear apart because of a will, that the law protects the legitimate children.

-Here is what will happen: we are going to submit an adoption file to the judge for children. There will be investigation lead by the welfare services. They will come here many times to see where and how the children live, they will ask them many questions, the children and you will even have to take some tests. There is no reason to worry, just be natural and answer with your heart. The teachers and the family doctor will be asked some questions too. You need to give the names of people who may write a letter of recommendation.

-Boudieu, are we going to be treated like criminals? What is everyone in the village going to think?

-Don't worry, Simone, interrupts the bishop, I will be your guarantee. I remember having lunch with Docteur Lerasle and I have met the teachers, they are your friends. There is also Yannick's father, a police officer is sworn, that will be another good point.

-I have studied your file with the bishop before we came, continues the priest, I don't see anything preventing your from adopting. It is only administrative.

-That's exactly what I am afraid of, administration, says Louis.

-I understand which is why I asked Father Bonafieu to take care of the file. He will walk you through every step, prepare the mail and will be with you every time you need him.

-What about the kids, when are we telling tem?

-Tomorrow, because we need to prepare them for all the visits and the questions. We also need to talk to everyone that will be interviewed by investigators.

-Well, I'm inviting everyone tomorrow night, so that you can explain better than we would.

-That's an excellent idea. Well, it is getting late, I'm going to bed.

Later in the room, Simone turns off the light and snuggles against her husband.

-Can you believe it, Louis? They are really going to be ours?

-Since the bishop took care of it and since he is here, I have no doubt.

-Then, the Lord really listens to our prayers!

-With a missionary daughter, He should listen to our prayers, and who know, maybe he wants one of our boys too.

-You talk like a non believer, He is not like that, He does not calculate like a peasant: I give you this, you give me that!

-Did you see how our Didier reacted? I'm so proud of him.

-You remember how he loved them as soon as Christine arrived ? How he was able to deal with Pascal and understand him.

-Can you believe it has been seven years already?

-Tell me about it, a few more days and Benoît will be going to do his military service.

-Stop that, you're so silly sometimes!

-That's why you love me, answers Louis, teasing her.

Heart's bonds

NOVEMBER 1982, LA FERME HAUTE

My dear daughter,

Your last letter was very short. I know that you don't tell us what is going on. It isn't smart from you because I worry even more not knowing and I imagine the worse.

You tell me that you won't be there, once again, for Christmas. Even though you tell us the same thing every year, I still cannot get used to it. I still expected it and sent you a few parcels these past weeks, since we never know what arrives at destination and what is misappropriated. You say that you are happy, but I know you and I'm quite sure that you must get angry from time to time. When I think that I complain about French administration, when I think about you, I feel ashamed.

It has been five months since we started the adoption procedure. It is a pain to have to go through every step, see all these people who don't know us but judge us, knowing that they can decide about our lot. Fortunately, Father Bonafieu is very calm, because the last time we saw the judge, I started being upset. Can you believe that she dared say that the children had the intellectual capacity to receive a high education and thus we were not the most suitable parents for them! That maybe they would be better off in a city with a family of executives rather than with farmers! If the Father had not been there, I think I would have strangled her.

I remember what you told us about the DASS. We met wonderful people, but also, for some of them, you would wonder if they have a heart when they say such things and pretend to care only for the children.

It is true that the children are very smart, and we didn't need their tests to know it. Pascal wants to be 'Pope or doctor' and Benoît 'police officer vet', how being raised in the country should be an obstacle to it? We are very capable of paying for their studies. I'm telling you, it hurts to feel like we are considered like dirt.

Apparently, when asked 'Describe for us the ideal family', both pitchouns said : 'ours' and when asked 'Imagine yourself in another family', they answered: 'We will get Godfather and Godmother married to-gether and we will live with them.'

And here is the judge asking us if we had heard about the questions and if we told the kids how they should answer!

Oh well, in spite of all this trouble, our file is supposed to 'run its course' and we should have an answer in a few months. I can't wait until everything is over, because I have knots in my stomach and your dad has lost his appetite.

The children seem to take it as a game and are looking forward to having the same last name as ours, Martin.

Here are some drawings, pictures and little words from the kids. As you can see, we think of you all the time and hope to see you soon.

I send you lots of hugs and kisses and everyone here does too.
Love

Mom

Heart's bonds

APRIL 1983, CHARTRES

The Martin family is very impressed as they arrive at the bishop house. For Didier, Pascal and Benoît, it is the first time they come to Chartres. Simone and Louis have not been there since Christine took her vows and became Sister Marie-Claire fifteen years ago. The bishop invited them for Easter weekend to celebrate the full adoption of the two boys. They chose this day to put a memory stone on Little laughing Flower's grave so that the boys can place it for their late parents; then they are going to visit the headquarter of the Little Sister of Saint Paul congregation and tomorrow, they will assist to the service celebrated by their godfather.

Father Emmanuel welcomes them:
-The bishop is very sorry, he was not able to come himself. I will show you your rooms, then I can take you for a visit of the cathedral. We are expected at 4:00 at the congregation, which leaves us some time.

The boys really like the young priest who often comes with their godfather. He is tall, jovial and smiling all the time. Since being 'the bishop's assistant' is very mysterious for them, they concluded that he must be his adopted son, and anyway, he usually says 'Father' instead of 'My Lordship.'

Father Emmanuel is passionate about the cathedral: its architecture and its history have no secret for him, but what he loves most about it is today's life, how it gathers so many people, how it attracts pilgrimages, how the youth community of Ile de France walks the 100 miles from Paris to there every year... The boys listen carefully, so amazed at everything they discover that they forget about time.

-Oh Lord, it is so late! We need to run! Suddenly says the priest looking at his watch.

As they arrive at the congregation of the Sisters of Saint Paul of Chartres, a beautiful surprise awaits them: Marie-Claire is by Bishop Benoît's side. The children run to her, overjoyed. They visit the common rooms of the convent, follow the main galleries, then go to a small room that was reserved for them. Simone and Louis, worried that they could not explain clearly enough the meaning of the stone for the grave, asked the bishop to explain it to the children. Sister Marie-Claire starts with something they already know: the war, their mother, Little Laughing Flower wounded, the sister's help, the arrival in France, her death after giving her children to the nun's care, her burial in the sisters graveyard, where they are going to go for the first time. The most important is to pray for her and not to forget her. Bishop Benoît goes on and tells them about their search with no success to find their father and reminds them of the different steps and investigations they undertook lately. He explains that their father is considered dead and that is why they will add a slab on their mother's grave. Finally now, Louis, Simone, Didier and Marie-Claire are officially their family, they will have the same last name, Martin, with all the love that it represents from everybody. Benoît jumps in Simone's arms.

-You're my mother for good now, forever!

Everyone cries either openly or more discreetly. Pascal did not say anything. He seems lost in his thoughts.

-Are you OK, brother? Asks Didier, putting his hand on the boy's head.

-Godfather, what is on the slab?

-Here it is, my boy.

'Pascal and Benoît thank Little Laughing Flower and their unknown father to have given them life and to have interceded to find them a new family. We will always love you.'

-What does interceded mean?

-Well, your biological parents asked Jesus to make everything all right and helped you become little Martins.

-It is not right. Jesus is not nice and God is not either. Tomorrow, I am not going to church!

-Pascal, what is going on? Why do you talk like this?

-Why is my mother dead? Why is Godmother so poor and so skinny with many children with no parents in my country where they do not even have enough to eat? And why has my father disappeared? Why do bad people win wars and good people die? Why do Benoît and I get to have a new family and new parents when so many others have nothing?

-Pascal, my boy, here are very deep

thoughts. Very intelligent people have wondered about that for centuries and we do not have an answer. But you are not right? Men do wars, they are the selfish ones, refusing their neighbour's love, which lead to chaos. We must believe that God is good, that He loves us, that Jesus is our saviour; the boys' godfather tries to reason him.

-What has triggered all these negative thoughts on such a day of joy? Asks Marie-Claire.

-In the galleries, there are plenty of photos: rice fields, people... I saw the pictures you sent us but those are different, they are huge. For the first time, I have imagined what my mother looks like; I understood that it was not you, that it will never be you, nor Mommy Simone. It is as if something broke all of a sudden in my heart.

-You are a smart and sensitive boy, it is a lot of emotion for you, I understand, but do you only know how much we love you, that all that matters for us is that you and Benoît are happy?

Simone is crying, she would never have imagined such a reaction. She wonders what she has done, or not done for the boy to react the opposite of what they expected. Louis does not say a word. He looks at one after another, trying to find a clue on what position to adopt. Benoît cries softly in Simone's arms, he does not understand what is going on, but he knows that all the joy has changed into tears.

Pascal is lost. It seems that everything collapses and that he spoiled the day.
-Son, I think we have a lot to talk about. If you do not go to church tomorrow, I will not be upset. You should know that I understand your feelings, but look around you, is that how you want to thank those, who love you, for what they have done to you?

Pascal sniffs and gives a kiss to Simone.

-Forgive me please; I did not want to hurt you. She takes him in her arms and kisses him with all her strength.

-You did not want to, but you did, says Louis reproachfully.

-Forgive me, Papa Louis.

-Boudiou, what have we done to God for him to give us such kids?

-And those, peuchère, we chose them!

Once everyone stopped crying and kissed one another, a certain peace came back and the little group finally goes to the grave where the boys lay the slab. After a blessing and a prayer, they have dinner at the bishop's place. Tonight, the feast becomes a quiet and oppressive dinner. Didier decides to sleep with the two boys, hoping that the reminder of their early childhood would bring them peace.

-We are sorry, My Lordship, to spoil your weekend like this. I am ashamed of what happened and I do not understand a thing.

-Louis, there is no reason to be ashamed. On the contrary, it is a good thing that it happened today and that Pascal was able to express himself. The trauma he went through as a baby was pouched deep inside of him. His survival instinct helped him adapt right away to his new life, forgetting the past. However, such a wound always has to come forward one day or another. We were so happy to see the two boys blossom that we too closed our eyes on their past. Nevertheless, all the love in the world is not enough; we have to live with reality. I know it is a paradox that it is when they are finally adopted, finally on your family record book that their need for identity and their bond with their biological parents appear. It is important that you do not see it as a rejection or a denial of your love for them. Benoît is lost, but he will follow his brother, it is only natural. Pascal became aware today of the existence of his parents. Until now, they had no more consistence than fairy tales characters. He will have to mourn them: he finds them and loses them all at once. Give him space to find his way; he will only love you more for that.

-But we will not know how to handle him, not how he will influence Benoît.

-Without a doubt, Simone, which is why, I think, you should see a psychologist to help you.

-They are going to think we are crazy, in our village!

-No, Louis, first, asking for help does not mean you are crazy, on the contrary. Second, you do not need to shout it around the village and let ignorant people misjudge you. Tell the teacher and Doctor Lerasle and that is it.

-My poor daughter, you came from the other side of the world to celebrate with us and now you must be disappointed!

-No, mom, do not worry. I think that bishop Benoit is right. Don't you always say that it is better to resolve a crisis than to let it grow?

-Except that here, we had no knowledge about it!

-We all wanted to forget, and I was the first one to, it is human nature. It takes even more love to be an adoptive parent than a biological one, more selflessness. We take more chance to be misunderstood, one day even rejected, but it is still worth living.

-Do you think that when they grow up, they will decide to go to Vietnam and abandon us? Asks Simone, nervous to think about it.

-They will eventually need to go there, to see, to smell, to feel, to understand... However, I hope that they will never stop loving you.

-What is the use of full adoption then, it cost us so much worries, to Louis and me?

-It is exactly like blood children, they too can go away.

-Just as you did, you even changed the pretty name that we gave you for your baptism!

-Do I love you less for that?

-Well, little Pascal may be right then: the Lord is not so nice after all.

-Simone, you should not say such thing in front of a bishop!

-I believe there is too much emotion here. Let us go to bed, we will start again tomorrow.

That night, Marie-Claire in her nun cell and bishop Benoît in his room spend the night praying.

Pascal holds Benoît asleep in his arm. He does not understand the anger he felt this afternoon. Those new feelings scare him. He feels ashamed, thinking of Simone's tears, of Louis' reproachful look and of his godparents' distressed ones. He made so many efforts to adapt, so that no one would call him the chink again, but he now realizes that the world is larger than Saissac, how many times would his little church fit in the huge cathedral? One year ago, when Shooting Star was born, life was so beautiful! When Louis and Simone told them that they were starting an adoption process, he felt like the king of the world. So why did everything shatter in front of pictures and a grave?

With tears in his eyes, Pascal says goodbye to his childhood, to the cocoon in which he grew up. At eleven, long before his body does, his spirit enters teenage.

Didier does not sleep either. He is hurt. Since the first day, he has loved those two brothers with all his heart. He felt responsible for Pascal right away and overprotected him like his child. They share the same passion for horses; they do not need to talk to understand each other. In Spite of the difference of age, he found the brother he had dreamt of. How did he not see this coming? Not anticipating the questions which darken Pascal's heart? Who is responsible? The investigators? Didier is trying to find who is guilty, who he can focus his anger on, his disappointment, his reproaches. He cannot and does not want to be angry at his brother. On this day, when the past should have been abolished, the past itself came for revenge like a boomerang, hitting them in the heart. Something broke, whatever happens, a cloud has darkened the horizon. The wounds of the body can heal but those made to the soul by words remain forever.

Simone cannot fall asleep. For years, she feared that someone would take the children away from her. Today, she is afraid that they might leave on their own, which is more difficult. Is that what life is all about? When we think we have reached happiness, it evades us, just like carried by a tidal wave, until it comes back unexpected and leaves again, polishing our hearts like little stones on a beach.

PART II

Heart's bonds

Los Angeles, July 1985

Betsy & the children

Los Angeles: City of Angels! Betsy looks at this impressive city from the plane.

Angels... Where are they today in these dozens of miles spread out in front of her? This is not a city, but the world in miniature with hundreds of churches of all possible denomination, the Mormon temple, the synagogues, the mosque, the Buddhist temples ... with its devils: money, poverty, drug hell, crime, prostitution. Also with its saints and its angels, usually simple unknown people, dedicated to a cause, sometimes recognized prophets, whose books and voice bring a message of love and hope. No, it is definitely not a city but dozens of cities and villages next to each other, sometimes mixed... What a difference with Visalia, the little town where she was born, lost in the orchard in central California!

On this day, in the beginning of July, Betsy thanks the Lord for her chance. Last month, to celebrate her diploma and her acceptance at UCLA, her father, a wholesaler in fruits and vegetables, invited her to come with him for a housewarming party given by his partner in Los Angeles. This is where she met Mr. Tran, a well-known architect. He was distant and cold but Betsy, sparkling with joy and youth, did not hesitate to talk to him when they were introduced to each other and she seized her chance. When she told him that she was studying French, the stone face of the Asian man lit up.

Heart's bonds

-Miss, are you free for a summer job?

-Yes, well it depends what type of job.

-I would like you to take care of my two sons. They are thirteen and ten years old. Your job will consist of giving them the best vacation of their lives. You will have a car and a limitless budget at your disposal. Of course, you will have to be able to account for everything. Your wages will be $2000 a month, if this suits you.

Just like in a fairy tale! With the salary he offers, she will make in three months what she was planning to make next year with a partial job. This way, she can devote herself to her studies, without a difficult job that does not pay on evenings and weekends... Perfect! A limo is waiting for her at the airport. She arrives in Beverly Hills in a beautiful villa and is introduced in Mr. Tran's office. He is stern again.

'Brrr...' Thinks Betsy, 'I wish his sons aren't like him. He makes me feel so uncomfortable.' However, she forces herself to smile.

-Thank you for coming, Miss Betsy, I will explain to you the situation before introducing you to my sons. As you may know, I am from Vietnam. I built many houses in Saigon for Americans and had good friends among my clients. When the city was taken, they managed to provide me with visas for my family and myself. I had a three year old boy and my wife was about to give birth to our second child. Both were supposed to meet me at the US Embassy. Right before the North Vietnamese take over, the city was full under attack. I waited in vain and when I went looking for them, the soldiers who accompanied me turned around under the enemy fire and I was evacuated almost by force.

Mr. Tran tells his story monotonously, as if he were detached from the event. Only when he mechanically wipes his glasses, does he show his trouble. Betsy listens, moved by the events, which she can imagine as they are exposed to her.

-It was ten years ago, I never saw my wife again. I spent all these years doing some research. A few months ago, I finally succeeded. The Americans never looked for my family. Some French nuns saved them. My wife and my son arrived in France. My wife was wounded when she gave birth to my second son. One of the nuns grew up in a small village. She took the children to her parents' farm and the social services closed their eyes to it. Mr. Tran wipes his glasses again and goes on.

-When I finally found them, I wanted to take them back, but the French authority was opposed to it. They want to do an investigation, a trial... The farmers adopted the children who are considered under French law as their legitimate children: what an absurdity! I do not speak French, but thanks to my lawyers, I was able to take the children here for the summer vacation. Moreover, I will never send them back.

Tran said those last words with such violence that Betsy shivers. He goes on.
-I am an American citizen, I have money. I can get the best lawyers. I will fight here in my country.

There is in his tone such defiance that the sympathy she started to feel for him at the beginning of his story melts away.

-Here is what I expect of you: you have three months to make my sons become real Americans. They must speak English, love this country and they will ask to stay. Only then can I win. You will do everything they want, take them to every theme park as many times as they wish. You will please them. The only thing I want you to impose on them is to speak English. Do you understand?

-Yes, Mr. Tran.

-Ah, one more thing, they have French names, Pascal and Benoît, we need to change that. We will call them Peter and Ben. In addition, I do not want them to be Catholics anymore. I count on you. Goodbye, Miss, I do not have anything more to say to you. James will take you now to the children.

Betsy gets up and follows the butler. Just like in a dream, her fairy tale turns into a nightmare. Her impression is amplified as she meets the kids: they are sitting next to each other, visibly worried and lost. She sympathises with those two little boys, who have been dragged around in life against their will, from Asia to Europe, from Europe to America... She loves them at first sight and feels a terrible resentment against Mr. Tran. She takes a decision: she will neither force them to love this country, nor force them to choose their father over the family who looked after them for ten years.

She will love them and will respect their will. Honest and direct, by nature, she explains to them their father's desire, without scaring them by saying that he wants to keep them at all costs, but she tries to underline how much he loves them, which is why he never stopped looking for them. She tries to make them understand but feels helpless to see the children so worried. However, she is warm and she can feel a connection with them.

The children talk about their life in Saissac, Pascal describes her cat Samaou. His father did not want him to take her with him but he misses her already. He tells her how, with his mare Shooting Star, he has won first prize at a competition in Carcassonne. Benoît talks about Prince, his pony and most of all about his Mommy Simone who he loves more than anything. He does not understand why she could not come. James interrupts the flow of revelation by inviting them to meet Mr. Tran at the dining room.

The maid serves a Vietnamese meal.

-Betsy, tell my father that our godmother, Sister Marie-Claire, took us to a Chinese restaurant in Carcassone to introduce us to our country's food.

-Speak English or be quiet! Snaps Mr. Tran with violence. And I do not want you to talk about that nun who sold my children to greedy peasants who wanted cheap labour.

-But, Mr. Tran, it seems to me that those people raised your children with love.

-Be quiet, you do not know anything! I do not pay you to contradict me. Teach them English and don't you mind what is absolutely none of your business!

The children do not understand a word they say, but the tone speaks for itself. Pascal looks at his father reproachfully and Benoît starts crying. Nobody is hungry anymore; the plates go back to the kitchen almost full.

Although each boy has a room with Betsy's in the middle, the boys insist to sleep together. They lost their eloquence of the afternoon. The young girl gives them a kiss and goes to bed, leaving the door ajar. Until late in the night, she can hear them murmur and cry.

'Bastard' she whispers thinking about Mr. Tran. Who does he think he is? What are a few drops of semen worth against ten years of love and care? Why does he despise those who welcomed and raised his children rather than being thankful? Betsy feels in her heart a great warmth towards the adoptive parents, about whom the children speak with such love. Being herself raised in the country and having a passion for horses, she feels closer to those French people at the other side of the world, than to this 'American citizen' under the same roof. When she thinks that, she thought he really wanted the boys to have 'the time of their lives', she now realizes he only plans to buy them, manipulate and use them to win his trial. What are his real motives? Betsy cannot see the love of a father in Mr. Tran's behaviour, a love such as her own father has for her.

The following day, as the three of them go downstairs for breakfast, Mr. Tran has already left for his office. Jack, a young and nice Afro-American man introduces himself.

-I am your chauffeur for the summer, Miss Betsy. My job is to drive you wherever you want. The only obligation is to come back every evening for dinner, unless otherwise arranged in advance with Mr. Tran. Where do you want to go today, Miss Betsy?

-I think that the first destination for the children will be Disneyland.

-At your service, Miss, I prepare the car and will be waiting for you.

-Thank you Jack, here are Peter and Ben.

-How do you do, says proudly Pascal who has learned English for a year at school already.

-Pretty good! And you Sir?

-Nice to meet you, says quickly Benoît, who does not want to be left behind.

When they arrive at the parking lot, the park is packed.

-Don't worry, Miss, look, Jack takes 4 pass out of his pocket, last week, Mr Tran ordered passes for every park in California: no worry, no waste of time in lines, you can go as many times as you want.

-How convenient!

-You will have to thank Mrs Anny, his assistant, for that. She is the one who thought about all of these details to make life easier for you. In addition, here is an envelope for each one of you, some cash for the meals and gifts and here is a debit card for you Miss. Let me whisper to you the code.

-Thanks, Jack. You can go now, let us meet when the park closes in front of the main entrance.

Heart's bonds

-But I have the order to escort and protect you.

-Come on, there's no danger here! Take the day off and we will tell no one.

-I am sorry Miss. If you do not want my company, I can stay a few feet behind and protect you from there.

-Ok Jack, do not take it personally! I just think that it will be easier for the kids because they practically speak no English. It is their first day; I want to devote my day to them.

-I understand then, I let you go your way. We will probably meet from time to time if you do not mind.

-Alright, thanks. Ok, boys, let me explain, there are five countries here: Frontier land, for explorers; Adventure land for Cowboys and Indians; Fantasyland for fairy tales, Main Street, where we are standing, which shows the US last century; and Future land, the country of the future. You need between four and six hours to do all the attractions of one country. We can either do one country of your choice today, or do one or two attractions in each country to give you a general idea.

-I want to do the cowboys and Indians! Shouts Benoît, all excited and impatient.

-I would rather do a little of everything, answers Pascal. But what about you, Betsy, what do you like best?

-Let's be efficient, if you trust me, here is what I suggest for today: first, we listen to Abraham Lincoln recite the Gettysburg Address, and then we walk down Main Street in an old car. Then we do one or two attractions in frontier land and go on with Adventure land. What do you think?

-Ok, answers the boys in unison, certain to have a good time.

During the whole first show, the children believe that Lincoln is an actor imitating a robot. They are flabbergasted when Betsy tells them that it is a real robot. When they go out, they run to a fire-fighter car and drive down Main Street at the sound of the bell, amazed to see Sleeping Beauty's castle. The waiting line for the Jungle River is 20 minutes long, but the way the line is organized, the setting, the sound effects, the good atmosphere and the sun make it seem shorter. The children enjoy their discovery of the jungle, the crocodiles, and the hippos. They can easily imagine themselves as explorers and 'believe for fun' that the guide has a real gun. After all, it smells like powder! Their trip barely finished, they hurry towards the Tiki room, the enchanted universe of the Hawaii Islands where the trees, the flowers, the birds and the insects gather for a magical concert.

-'It's the tikiti tikiti tikiti ki room, where the birdies sing and the flowers bloom...' sing Pascal and Benoît together when they leave the place, their head full of colours and of the sounds of the tom-tom.

-Well, boys, are you hungry? Asks Betsy in English.

-What does it mean asks Benoît?

Pascal knows the answer and says it to his

brother proudly.

-Very good Pascal, but you see, you need to give time to your brother to think. He needs to guess what I asked, he will learn faster. When you learned French, nobody translated for you, just like any child, you had to guess, to associate words and gestures and you learned the language naturally.

-Yes, but a child needs a long time to learn.

-A baby understands already many things after a few months, and he has so much to discover. For you, it is easier. I will try to speak more slowly but more and more often in English, with short sentences, so that you can guess. All right? What do you want to eat? She asks in English.

-Yes, I am hungry, answers Benoît in French. Pascal laughs.

-Don't laugh. It is a good start, but not exactly that.

-Where do you go for lunch? Tries to guess Benoît again.

-OK, Pascal, your turn.

Heart's bonds

-What do you want to eat!

-Here we are! Says Betsy, as the children look puzzled.

-Where are we? What do you mean?

-It is just an expression, it means: yes, it is good; you found it, depending of the context.

-And in which context do we eat? Worries Benoît.

Betsy lowers her head and gives him a kiss.

-Come on boys, what about hamburgers?

-Hamburgers, yes, and fries!

-Good Ben: Hamburgers and French fries!

After their meal, they go to the Pirate of the Caribbean. The boys love it so much that they go three times in spite of the long line across the castle, the different jails and other settings making the time fly by. After their last turn, a tall pirate with a scary mask captures the boys.

-How much do you give me for these hostages?

-Jack, I recognize your voice, laughs Betsy.

When he heard the name, Pascal takes out the mask of his kidnapper and all start to laugh.

-Can I have a costume like this one? Asks Pascal.

-Of course, let us have a look at the shop.

-'Of course' means yes comments proudly Benoît who understood the tone.

-Of course underlines Betsy means 'bien sûr' in French.

The hands full of tunics, belts, large hats, swords, knife and guns, the two boys only need a mask that can only be found in adult size. Oh well, they have a fine look already and start right away to fight with elegance.

-Let's hurry, otherwise, we will miss the parade, says Jack.

When they arrive in front of the castle, they cannot get close enough to see the show. Jack grabs Benoît and puts him on one shoulder and Pascal on the other one. This way, the boys can see all the characters, the acrobats, the jugglers and the floats. When the chauffeur puts them on the floor after the show, they run after the end of the procession. Betsy drags everyone in a small shop on Main Street to drink a hot chocolate and eat cookies before it is time to go. The only thing that comforts the children when they leave the magical Kingdom is that they will be back the next day for other adventures. In the car, Betsy teaches them a few sentences to thank their dad and tell him about their day.

After a bath and putting on their nightclothes, the boys go to the dining room. Unfortunately, their father's coldness stops their attempt to communicate and the sentences they learned cannot come out of their mouth. Betsy starts to narrate the day.
-Thank you, but I do not need the details. I just want to be sure that they had a good day and that their English is getting better, which I cannot see yet, interrupts Mr. Tran. The rest of the dinner continues almost in silence.

In the evening, Pascal confides to Betsy:

-My whole life I prayed to find my father, but I do not want this one! He does not know how to hug, how to laugh. He scares me. He is mean.

-No, don't say that, didn't you spend a wonderful day, thanks to him?

-Not thanks to him, thanks to you, Jack, and the woman who bought the tickets.

-But your father paid for them.

-It does not matter! In addition, did you see how he talks to you? Who does he think he is?

-He is a great architect, very well known, he builds the houses of famous stars in Hollywood, he has many offices with many employees who respect him and depend on him. You should be proud.

-Daddy Louis and Mommy Simone have the bed & breakfast with the best reputation in the area. People come from far away: from Paris, Belgium and even Holland to taste their food. Didier is the best horseback riding instructor in the whole world and the nicest big brother ever, I am proud of them!

-Me too, and our godfather has the most beautiful cathedral and our godmother is the nicest in the whole universe.

-You will come and see us when we are back in France, you will see that we are not lying to you, continues Pascal.

-Mommy Simone is the best huggers, I am sure you never had one like that before. You will see, I will ask her to give you one.

Betsy has a lump in her throat. She can feel the love between the children and their adoptive parents and her heart bleeds just thinking that they may never see them again. She says she is very tired and goes quickly in her room before tears come down flowing on her cheeks.

During the next two weeks, life goes on from park to park, from beach to beach. Pascal wants to have fun. For him, it is a great chance to go to Disneyland, to discover the Far West at Knott's' Berry 'Farm, to ride on horses, to sail down the coast and visit the movie studios. He is fascinated by everything he sees and tries seriously to learn English. He always has thousands of questions and Betsy tries to answer them the best she can. He wants to learn how to surf and is amazed by the champions' performances. He is attracted to the Californian blond girls, especially to Betsy. He could do anything to please her.

Mr. Tran allows Betsy to go to the South for two days, to visit Sea World and the zoo in San Diego. The boys were in awe watching the orca, the dolphins, the California seals and the birds. They fish some pearl oysters in a tank and are amazed at the jewellery store. They choose a beautiful cross, made out of small pearls for their godmother, a heart shaped broach for their Mommy Simone, a mother of pearl cross to hang on the wall for their godfather. Betsy refuses the beautiful and expensive necklace they want to give her, but accepts a pretty keychain. They also give one to Jack who has tears in his eyes, moved by their nice gesture. In the evening, they have dinner in the Mexican quarter. The boys buy cowboy boots. They want to bring some back to Didier but do not know his size; they agree on a hat and a belt with a huge silver buckle representing a rodeo. For Daddy Louis, they choose a beautiful knife. They want to buy American saddles, but Betsy dissuades them because of the luggage restriction in a plane. In the motel, the pool opens until midnight and they all enjoy it, the adults as well as the children.

The day in the San Diego zoo is a beautiful and long dream day. On the way back, the children sleep in the car.

After the excitement about seeing something new every day, the children start to feel the weight of being far away from their family. Every day, the boys write a card to their adoptive parents and others to their godmother, godfather and their friends. Of course, Betsy brings them to the post office without hesitation, in spite of her boss' strict orders of keeping them from contacting anyone.

Pascal starts to tire from attraction parks and prefer lying on the beach. Benoît has become increasingly anxious. Although he is easily amazed by their daily adventures, he refuses to speak one word of English to his father, leaves his plate in the evening mostly full and cries every night. He buys toys, has a box full of treasures from the Far west, covers his bed with stuffed animals but does not spend one day without asking at least eight times: 'When are we going back to Mommy Simone and Daddy Louis?'

Betsy is neither a doctor, nor a psychologist but she has enough heart to see that his behaviour becomes more worrisome every day. She opens up to Mr. Tran who gets angry, call her 'sentimentally weak', threatens to fire her and replace her by someone more energetic, more capable to 'tame a difficult child.' That night, Betsy cannot sleep. In the morning, she takes her decision: she will go to the French authorities and look for help there.

In the morning, one thing is sure: she needs Jack to drive them and must be sure that he will not say a word. She cannot lie because if he accepts and Mr. Tran knows about it, he will lose his job. She waits for the car to be far from the house and says:

-Jack, I have a great favour to ask from you.

-Whatever you want, Miss Betsy.

-Even if that puts your job at risk?

-Must I drive 100 mph to thrill you? Teases Jack.

-No, take us somewhere without ever telling Mr Tran, even if you are tortured.

-Are you kidding?

-Not at all. I need to be sure that you will not say a word about where we went.

-You are having me worried with your conspiring look, but if I have to choose between you and Mr Tran, it is not fair: I would rather see your beautiful eyes and your smile than his dollars.

-Thanks, I knew I could count on you. Jack, take us to the French consulate.

-Are you leaving with the children?

-No, but I am worried for Ben, and I want to find someone who can help me.

-It is true; the little boy does not seem to be feeling well in the morning, or the evening, or even during the day. He is a good boy. Well, if you think that someone can help, I drive you there.

At the consulate, Betsy is surprised by the warm welcome they receive. After she explained why she has come to the assistant, they wait for a moment before being introduced to the consul himself. He listens to her, thanks her and asks to see each boy alone, one after the other. One hour later, he calls Betsy in his office.

-Miss, you were right to come to us. These children are by law under the French authority, since their father is only using his visitation right, in the midst of his process to be recognized as their father and named the children's only guardian. It is only natural that the social worker of our consulate visits the family. If I understand correctly, their godfather is the Chartres bishops. He is a friend the Los Angeles one, who told me about the strange story of these children. This brings weight to our intervention. Of course, we will not talk about your visit, you have nothing to fear. Thank you again.

Two days later, at dinner's time, the consulate assistant rings at Mr Tran's door without notice. Surprised but polite and always respectful of authorities, Mr Tran invites him at their table. In the following weeks, he receives an order from the French services abroad to take the children for a medical and psychological exam. Mr Tran, furious, calls his lawyer, who confirms that this process is completely legal, since the children are minors and French; Mr Tran is not yet recognize as their father and according to law, is only using a visitation permit as long as the trial to recognize his rights has not taken place. Having no choice, he asks Betsy to drive the children for the 'stupid and useless' tests.

The results are no surprise: Pascal's health is excellent, his psychological evaluation is normal; however, Benoît is at the breach of anorexia and depression. The doctors are clear: it is the child's best interest to go back to France in his family as soon as possible. In rage, Mr Tran has no choice but to let him go.

Although he cannot directly accuse Betsy

of intruding with the French authorities, he takes her responsible for the failure. With only Pascal at home, he sets in him all of his hopes, but also all of his expectation. Since Benoît is gone, he insists that 'Peter' goes with him to the office, as well as on the construction sites several times a week. He wants to impress him, show him what a great architect he is, why his son should be proud of him. He believes that Betsy is responsible for Ben's leaving, he only uses her as an interpret and reproaches her constantly Peter's lack of progress in English.

At the beginning, Pascal is flattered by the attention that his father shows him. He is amazed by the glass building, the great angle office on the 36th floor, the respect the employees show, the numbers of architects on a huge set. The models and the projects fascinate him. He strives to speak English, but his father's correcting him after each little mistake paralyses him and he makes much less progress than when alone with Betsy. Very quickly, he feels lost in a universe that is not his, in the middle of adults he does not understand. Business quickly requires Mr Tran's all attention and he becomes tired of having the boy next to him at all time. He noticed his interest for models and ask some employees to take care of Pascal who tries his very best to help at the models department.

Pascal, unhappy from his brother leaving him, disappointed from his father's disinterest, upset to see how he treats Betsy; soon acts like Benoît did before being sent back to France. Betsy is the first one to realize it and she easily understands why he changed like this. This time, she does not need to intervene. The consulate services follow closely now the evolution between the boy and his father. They allow him to stay the two months initially granted but persuade Mr Tran's lawyer that he needs to send back the boy at due date, unless he wants to put his trial at high risk.

On the day Pascal leaves, Mr Tran shows to Betsy all of his anger.

-Miss, you have been unworthy of the trust I had placed in you, you have accomplished nothing I asked you to, and you even set up my children against me...

In rage, Betsy does not let him continue.

-How can you say such a thing? What did you imagine? That your children were pieces of art that you only need to buy? No, you cannot buy love; it needs to be built, stone by stone, such as a cathedral in a man's heart. You only imposed your will, your desire. You wanted them to make efforts. Have you even tried to understand them? Have you learned a single word of French? Don't you have a heart keeping you from understanding the bonds they share with those who raised them and loved them for ten years? You do not deserve them...

-Get out! Get out at once; I do not want to see you anymore! Answers Mr Tran, white with rage, as nobody ever dare to talk to him like that.

Betsy leaves shaken, without thinking for a second about the wages he owes her. She walks away, alone, by foot, with her eyes full of tears. One block away, Jack reaches her by car.

-Miss Betsy, you do not think I will let you leave like this, I hope; where can I drive you?

-Thank you Jack, I am going to UCLA campus, but I do not want you to lose your position.

-Don't worry, hop in. Dry your pretty eyes, Miss, I bet you will see your boys again. They like you, especially Peter; he is in love with you.

-You are kidding! He is just a boy!

-Exactly, at that age feelings are greater and more beautiful.

-You are so nice, you had me smile!

-I will not forget you either, Miss. It was a pleasure to go out like this, the four of us; the kids are precious. One day, we will have a big party altogether!

-May God hear you!

TOULOUSE BLAGNAC AIRPORT

Pascal is proud of himself. His godfather went to the airport in Paris to welcome Benoît and then drive him to La Ferme Haute, but Pascal thought he was able to change flight and take another plane to go to Toulouse. In Roissy, he had to get his luggage to go through custom. A little boy with a full cart intrigued the police. They asked many questions. Betsy made sure to have his bags and suitcase taped, they did not ask him to open them and let him check in for Toulouse. With Benoît, they agreed that he would keep the gifts so that they could give them together. They were afraid that the beautiful knife they bought for pap Louis might be confiscated.

Barely out of the plane, he runs as fast as he can: they are all here! He jumps into Daddy Louis' arms.

-My Daddy Louis, I missed you so much!
-What about me? I count for nothing? Ask Simone.
-The poor boy only has two arms! Retorts Louis, proud to have been the first to hug the boy.

Pascal kisses his Mommy Simone, Didier, Benoît and his friend Yannick who came to welcome him. It is a joyful little group who gets the luggage, then go into the car. On their way to La Ferme Haute, everyone has many questions for him. Pascal can barely answer them all at once, but everybody laughs. When they arrive, Pascal runs towards the house and calls his cat.
-Samaou, Samaou.

She is lying on his bed. Simone arrives:

-You know, she was so sad, we thought she was letting herself die. She did not want to eat, refused to go out of your room. It was great time that Benoît came back, it looked like she understood that if one was back, the other would follow one day. But the poor animal, she was so worried. If you go back, it is sure, she will die.

-Don't worry, Mommy Simone, we will not leave you again.

Samaou puts her paws around the child's face, hides her head under his chin and purrs so loudly that she starts drooling. Pascal feels good. Holding tenderly his cat, he snuggles in the arms of the person who loves him most. He puts his head on Simone breast and hears her heart beat with joy.

- Now, let us go see Shooting Star!

Still holding Samaou, the child goes to the stables. His mare smells him and neighs as soon as he comes. He puts the cat down, she curls around his legs, and the boy pats his horse.

Heart's bonds

-What about you, pretty one, did you miss me?

For her answer, she gives him a tap of her head.

-I knew I would find you here.

The boy turns around. Didier looks at him with a great smile. Around him are Benoît and Yannick. Pascal breathes deeply, filling his lungs with the smell of straw and horse sweat, he smiles. 'Here is my family, here is my kingdom' he tells himself happily.

Heart's bonds

SEPTEMBER 1985, LA FERME HAUTE

My dear daughter,

We have finally our angels back. They sure made me shed tears, those two, but I'm not being fair, the joy they have brought me are way greater than the worries and I would not hesitate for one-second if I had to do it again.

Guess what? They brought a gift for every-one. You know me, I first said I wanted nothing that was bought with that Mr Tran's money, but they started crying, they said it was their own money since it was given to them. Your father and Didier were on their side and I found myself like an idi-

ot. I must say that their gifts are beautiful; it is moving to see how well they chose each gift for each one of us. Of course, we keep yours here for when you come because we cannot trust the mail.

You know that Pascal had a difficult time since that sad day in Chartres, well; his trip put back his thoughts into place. He has never been this affectionate with us. As for Benoît, forgive me once more, but this one is his Mommy Simone's little boy.

I don't know what the future holds for us, because we still have a trial in front of us, so please, since you know how to pray, I count on you and your friends to tell the Lords that those little ones want to stay with us. You understand, so you may find the words to convince Him.

Write back soon, give us news and most important, tell us when you think you can come to France. I send you kisses from us all.

Your Mom

PS: the boys said they sent you plenty of cards from America, did you receive them?

Heart's bonds

LOS ANGELES, SEPTEMBER **1985**

One of the villas Mr Tran is currently working on, is for the famous psychologist John Polsky. A fine humanist, deeply moved by neighbour's love, he senses the family disequilibrium when his architect introduced him to his son Peter. By his cold tone when Mr Tran answers: 'He is in France', after John asks for news, Polsky cannot help but offer his services. He does it tactfully and with conviction, so that Mr Tran listens.

The first months are hopeless. John does not find any possible entry in the frozen case he faces. No patient has been so difficult, so hard to get through. His shell is so thick that he seems stranger to any form of warmth. John is going through his first failure in his carrier. His only hope lies in the fact that Mr Tran keeps coming to him, weeks after weeks.

Heart's bonds

VIETNAM, OCTOBER **1985**

My dear family,

I am both happy to know the children back to you and sad that their experience with their father was unsuccessful, especially with Benoît. You can count on us to pray for the judge to choose the best solution for the children; unfortunately, we should not lie to ourselves: birth parents usually win against adoptive parents. The difference in our case is that the children are legally adopted and usually there is no going back to a judgement. Our case is new, which is why there is no way of knowing.

I received a long letter from His bishop Benoît. He loves our godsons very much. I know that he is in contact with a lawyer specialized in 'children's rights' at UNESCO. We will do anything that can be legally done to show the boys' best interests. What else can be said: Let us have faith.

My dear mom, I know you well enough to imagine how concerned you are because of the trial. I count on our friend, Doctor Lerasle, to take care of your health: do not get sick, which would do no good, on the contrary. Of course, I can hear you from here answering that it is easy for me to say that... You see, I smile just thinking about it. Believe me, I understand, it is easy for none, especially not for Didier and Dad who act tough but who would go to the moon to please Pascal and Benoît.

Sister Anh and Sister Dao join every day in my prayers. They have not forgotten those tragic days in April 1975 and are affected by all this.

We were lucky to have the children for ten years. God knows what will happen in the following months, but what is for sure is that nobody, nothing will ever erase all the happiness and the love shared. Those heart bonds you have created will never be destroyed, may this truth bring you peace in these difficult moments.

I hug and kiss you all. God bless you.

Sister Marie-Claire

LA FERME HAUTE, NOVEMBER 1985

-Godfather, Godfather! The two boys run to the car when they see the bishop arrive. The hugs are even warmer than usual.
-Give him space to get into the house, it is cold as hell outside and it is pouring!

Bishop Benoît and Father Emmanuel find refuge into the house, already being wet after the few yards they walked to get in.
-The rooms are warm, go get changed. I prepare coffee for you to warm up.
-Thank you Simone, we should call you Saint Martha.
-It is not nice of you to tease me, Bishop!
-I am not teasing you, it is a compliment. You are always taking care of everybody's

wellbeing. You are right, we are going to change clothes and we will be back in a few minutes.

Pascal follows his godfather.
-I need to talk to you alone.
-Is it urgent?
-Well, I have been meaning to ask you this for months, I am a little impatient.
-Come in, you can well see me put on a sweater instead of my jacket. What is so important?
Pascal breathes deeply and starts:
-Well, for years, I prayed and I promised the Lord that if I found my father, I would become a priest; but the one He gave me does not suit me at all. Do I still need to become a priest?

The bishop looks at the child tenderly.
-Come on sit on the bed. The bishop takes a chair and sits in front of Pascal.
-Listen to me; we do not trade with God. He is not a friend, who you give this to get

that. It does not work like this. Our Father in Heaven asks us a pure heart and our love, freely given, not against any obligation. One does not become a priest to thank Him for a prayer He granted. It is a long road, a call to which you answer. Give me a few good reasons to enter the order.

-Father Emmanuel is the happiest man on earth, he told me so. He thinks there is no greater joy on earth than giving one's life to God and to one's brothers.

-I think so too, but what about you?

-I want to be like you and make many priests happy.

-You are flattering me, but it is not a good enough reason. Do you feel you are called?

-I do not know.

-If you are one day, you will know.

-But I have a problem...

-Tell me.

-Well, it is my secret, you won't tell anyone?

-I promise.

-I want to get married with Betsy, but she probably will not accept me because I am too short.

-How old is she?

-18 or 20, I am not sure.

-Then in ten years or so, if she is still free and you still love her, you can tell her. It is OK if she is a little older.

-But I will still be too short! She is a tall American and I am a small Vietnamese.

The bishop makes great efforts not to laugh.

-Give yourself some time. If things are meant to be, they will, love has nothing to do with size. However, if you already think about getting married, you cannot also think about becoming a priest.

-That is exactly what worries me. So, you are sure, I don't have the obligation to become a priest?

-I relieve you from your promise, is that better?

-Thank you Godfather.

-Don't thank me. Let us go, Simone must be worried not to see us.

Year after year, the bishop enjoys more and more spending a few days in Saissac. He recovers from the stress put on his shoulders by his charge of souls. His hosts' simplicity and kindness, the exuberant love his godsons show him ease the difficulties and the weight of his responsibilities. Since he became his assistant, Father Emmanuel has not missed one of these trips, sharing the joys but also the worries that the trial for fatherhood brought. Although they had always been in favour of the 'birth right' and the necessity of giving back children to their own family when it was found, they changed position as they were confronted to reality: a relationship woven for ten years cannot be cut all of a sudden, and language and cultural issues cannot be ignored. More important than the parent's rights, are the children rights. On the international scene, the higher good of the children has recently been reconsidered, it is now an important part of the decision, the child has become'thinking individual' and not an object anymore. The negative experience last summer, although more intense for Benoît than Pascal, convinced the bishop to use all of his power in the procedure, so that the biological father would be acknowledged but the children should be free to choose where they want to live. That is what he wants to explain during his visit, without giving them false hope: it will be difficult; the American lawyers are dreadful opponents. A rich American against French peasants, the weight of money against years of love; the self-control made in Asia against the demonstration of a Southern 'mama': who will win?

Simone prepared a goose casserole, with a large salad. Louis opened a bottle of Fitou, a nice wine from the South, a mix of three different grapes, a symbol of the local cuisine. Everybody enjoys the meal. The children tell their vacation, speak about Betsy and Jack with warmth, and explain their ill at ease with the one they still want to call 'Mr Tran.'

Once the children put in bed, bishop Benoît has a long conversation with Simone, Louis and Didier, explaining to them what he has done so far, his hopes and his fear.

-If he takes the children from us, I am going to kill him!
-Simone, calm down, do you think you could be very useful to the children from jail? Asks the bishop, accustomed to the figures of speech his host uses.
-And I will kidnap them! Says Didier, who does not want to stay out of the conversation.
-Good Lord, bishop, what do you want me to do between those two? Grumbles Louis.
-First, you will not say these kinds of stupid things in front of the judge. You have to understand, he does not care about what

you think and what you feel: his job is to find out the best interest for the children.

-It does not take a rocket scientist to understand that the children will only be happy with us, interrupts Didier.

-Probably, but I do not forget that other judge who thought the children were too smart for us and asked me if I did not think they would be better off in a city, in a family of executives, continue Simone. She made me crazy, even though at that time, their father did not ask for them, none did.

-Simone is right. We have to be ready for any possibility. Just like last time, we will ask Doctor Lerasle and Yannick's father to talk to the judge. May be even the school's director? What do you think?

Father Emmanuel takes note of every possible witness, as well as every good idea coming from here or there to give weight to the file he will be giving to the lawyers. It is late at night when everyone goes to bed.

Simone snuggles into Louis' arms:

-Please, tell me that the kids are not going to the other side of the world where we will never see them again.

-I know it is what you want to hear. Let me tell you one thing: if God has some time to study the question, He will put in the judge's brain that the kids' best interest is to be loved, so that he will understand that they need to be with us.

-God may not have time to take care of everyone, but a bishop should be heard, don't you think?

-Come now, sleep, darling. I promise you that everything will be all right.

Heart's bonds

Los Angeles, December 1985

-Mr Tran, I have just received this information. Although we have an international right file, the trial will take place in France. All of our attempts have failed to have it held in the US. It will take place on January 4th. Can you do the trip?

There is a silence.

-Mr Tran?

-Yes, I will be there. I ask my assistant to be in contact with your office so that we can travel together. I hope you are ready.

-Absolutely. Two associates are coming with us. They speak fluently French and are experts in international rights.

-I expect nothing less of your firm. Good-night.

He hangs up the telephone, stands up and goes to the window. The sky is dark, smog covers the city. Although it happens often, Lee Tran is angry about it. He does not like this time of year. He finds ridiculous the snowmen painted on the windows, the Christmas tree under the Californian sun, the fake Santa Claus walking around the city. He cannot stand the sugary carols on the radio, the crowd in the stores, all these people running around, and these festivities, which only remind him how lonely he is. At that moment, he hates the occidentals, their civilization of pleasure, money. They robbed him of everything: his life, his country, his family. He will have his revenge; he will bring back his sons! Where? Here? He looks at his office; the model of his latest mall in discussion sits in the corner. He closes his eyes. He can see the rice fields on the road leading to his grandparents' house, Saigon before the war, Little Laughing Flower... His mind wanders; he can see his friend, Bert, arms open, his friendly smile. He can feel inside the wrench that hurt so much that he never lets a chance to come to the surface. He opens his eyes, rubs his face with his hands, pulls himself together, sits at his desk and takes the phone:

-Miss Anny, ask Don and Steve to come up with the latest changes to the project.

Work is the drug that allows him to live.

CHRISTMAS 1985, LA FERME HAUTE

A surprise awaits the children on Christmas Eve. Their godfather's car, driven by Father Emmanuel, parks in the farmyard: coming out of the door is not the Bishop but their godmother. Simone managed to keep secret her visit, which both makes her happy and concerned. Sister Marie-Claire was repatriated by plane because of a serious infection. After some time in Chartres hospital, she is sent to Saissac for recovery for several weeks. She was in no condition to drive, which is why the bishop put his car and chauffeur at her disposal. Father Emmanuel was happy of the mission and contacted the local priest to co-celebrate the different services during that week of feast. Simone runs to take her daughter in her arms.

-Oh God, you only have the skin and the bones left!

-Don't worry, Mom, I am all right, I am only very cold.

The children are shy with their godmother, lying down on the big sofa, wrapped in blankets, with a pale face, empty cheeks with huge and dark eyes circles. She is smiling but tears run down her cheeks. They kiss her. Pascal gets his cat and puts her on his godmother's lap.

-Samaou will keep you warm and she will fetch me if you need anything.

-I am sorry to spoil your Christmas.

-Nonsense! How can you say such a thing? For sure we would have like it better if you were healthy, but I'd rather have you sick here, close to me, than at the other side of the world. This is our first Christmas together since you entered the orders.

-Don't worry, Sister Marie-Claire, I will do

one service here, just for you.

-You will do it here. Can we be there too?
Wonders Pascal.

-Yes, but first you will have to go to church
in Saissac; because you are not sick, then if
you want to be there for a second one, you
are welcome.

After resting the whole afternoon, warmed
up thanks to the chimney but most of all
thanks to the love around her, Marie-Claire
manages to sit at the table. She eats little
and asks for rice, which Simone finds
disappointing, but she still cooks some for
her. Benoît goes to the kitchen with her:

-Why are you crying, Mommy Simone?

-Because I have been peeling onions.

-No, that was this afternoon, is that because
you are afraid Godmother may die?

-Who can put such ideas in your head, if
she heard you, what would she say?

-I am scared too.

Simone holds him tight in her arms.

-Benoît, my love, do not be afraid, it is

Christmas, nothing sad can happen. She is very ill but she will recover, we will take good care of her.

-Promise?

-Go now, sit with them.

Looking at his tired sister, Didier starts saying:

-I bet you are as light as a feather. I am taking you to bed and I will stay with you and read for you, just as you did when I was a child.

-You certainly will not be the one to help her get undressed and wash.

-Let him come with me, Mom, I will manage and I will be happy to spend some time with my little brother.

-Who is taller than you are by far! Adds Didier laughing.

Pascal and Benoît are happy to share the room. They will spy on Santa Claus, who they do not believe in anymore, but Louis keeps putting on the costume and puts the gifts at the foot of the tree, delighting everyone.

In the morning, amongst the gifts, Sister Marie-Claire finds the little cross, made of pearls.

-Oh thank you, my darlings, it is beautiful! With your love around my neck, I am certain to get better!

It is snowing: snowflakes cover the ground and turns even the dustbins into beautiful immaculate mounts. The family stays by the fire in the living room. Each one enjoys that peaceful moment of quietness, the roasted chestnuts and the tangerine skins thrown on the live embers fill the air with a 'Christmas perfume', which warms the heart. Marie-Claire is sleeping in the comfortable chair; the rest of the family is playing with the new board games received in the morning, trying to make as little noise as possible, not to wake her up. Father Emmanuel left in the beginning of the afternoon. The private mass he served brought peace to everyone, giving hope and confidence in the future.

A few days later, the nun takes advantage of gaining a little more strength to talk with her godsons. They are disappointed that she did not receive any card they sent her. After hearing about everything, they did and seeing all the gifts they brought back, she points out:

-It seems like your father spoiled you, why aren't you thankful for that?

-Because he is mean, answers right away Benoît.

-How can you say that sweetheart?

-First, he changed our names and he does not speak any French!

-That is not a good reason, billions of people speak other languages! He hired Betsy so that you could communicate.

-No, he wanted us to speak English; he did not want her to translate.

-It is a way to teach, it is not that bad.

-He asks us to say Sir in each sentence. Who does he think he is, the king or what?

-It is just a way to speak in English, a sign of respect.

-Leave it Benoît; you do not know how to explain. In fact, he does not love us. He did not hug or kiss us once.

-It sure changed you from Mom who cannot stop giving you hugs, but look at Dad, he is not really expressive.

-Oh, that is not the same. Daddy Louis has always taken good care of us: he teaches us so many things, he repairs our bikes, he makes toys for us, he offered me Shooting Star and Prince to Benoît. He is always there when we need him, he understands us, and he has a way to pat our hair with his hand or put it on our shoulder that says how much he loves us.

-You can read it in his eyes, his look, and his smile. Nothing of that with Mr Tran!

-Listen kids, your father is Vietnamese. Asian dads do not take care of their children the way we do in France, it is a different culture. He probably never learned. He only knew war when he was your age.

-But he has been in the US for ten years. Betsy told us about her dad, he is just like Daddy Louis!

-I understand that you feel better here, you grew roots, you are pampered, and life is easy, simple. You are right to love our parents because they are wonderful, but I'm only asking you to make room in your heart for your father as well. Remember when you were very little, I asked you to pray for him; well now do not reject him. Try to understand him. He looked for you for ten years, isn't that a proof of love?

-He wanted to find 'Little Laughing Flower', not us.

-Pascal, it is not nice to say that, he looked for his whole family, you three.

-He hates me because my mom died when I was born.

-Benoît, do not think like that. I told you before, a bomb killed your mother and it was a miracle that we saved you. You have nothing to do with it and your father knows that. He was happy to know that you are alive and that you are a boy.

-In any case, we are lucky you brought us here, I would not have been happy if he had raised us. Here, we have a mother, a father, a big brother, a godfather, a godmother, friends... You are the family we love.

-I love you too, but there is going to be a trial. We do not know what the judge will decide. You have to be ready to go back to America with your father.

-No, the judge gave us to Mommy Simone and Daddy Louis, we are Martin now!

-I know Benoît, it was three years ago, for your adoption, but then, he did not know that your father lived and was looking for you.

-I will always stay with Mommy Simone or I will die!

-Don't say such terrible things!

-And I will leave with Shooting Star and Samaou and nobody will ever find me!

Heart's bonds

-Darlings...

Sister Marie-Claire starts crying. The children are embarrassed.

-Don't cry, we did not want to hurt you!

She holds her tight in her arms.

Los Angeles, February **1986**

Doctor John Poslky's practice

Mr Tran enters the office:

-The judgement was given. They recognize me as the father but I was denied the custody of the children. I have visitation rights and I can take them on vacation for three weeks but I cannot leave the French soil with them without a special authorisation of the judge. My children will stay with the Martins until they are 16, and then they can choose if they want to live with me. They also keep their French names until they are 18, they can decide then the name and nationality they want to have. I do not understand you, the occidentals. In our country, a child obeys, he belongs to his father and we do not have to ask him any question or do as he wants. A son does what a father asks, parents choose spouses for their children, their studies, their job. I have two sons to take on my company after me, to carry my name and with your laws; they are called Martin and will become farmers!

It is the first time that he pronounces the name of the adoptive parents. He always said: 'the farmers' with despise. John says no word. He is waiting. Suddenly, the miracle he had been waiting for happens: Mr Tran starts crying. Softly at first, then abundantly, without a word... John looks at the shell opening in front of him. As if each teardrop is taking one piece of stone after the other... he cries for a long time...

John keeps quiet and observes in silence, out of respect, of compassion. It is no more 'Mr Tran, the difficult client, the week chore' in front of him, but a man broken by sadness. He is the symbol of misunderstanding between men. John starts praying; fervently ... several hours go by.

-I am so sorry, I should not have let myself go like this, and it is the first time.

-Lee, don't you know that it is through its cries and screams that a newborn show it is alive? Don't you know that a man can be reborn several times? I have been waiting for this moment for a long time! Be proud of your tears, thanks to them, a new life opens in front of you. I will help.

-I am drifting away.

-Lee, the coast never floats to the boat. It is for the captain to bring it to port. Take back the steering wheel. Be confident. Do you know the story of the two prisoners in the same jail? One always looked at the bars; the ground in the yard, the other looked between the bars and admired the sky. The first one drowned in despair, whereas the second one rose, because he knew that he was free, since nothing could impede his spirit and his heart. It is usually very difficult to change the circumstances imposed on us, but we are master of the way we see them. The way we see, things determine our thought, thus our emotions. It is a spiral. You choose to go up or down. Lee, I will help you change the way you look at the situation. Come now, it is late, let us have dinner.

Mr Tran is too broken by his emotions to react, but he finds the strength to notice:
-John, I meant to tell you, it has been years since anyone called me Lee.
-Because it has been years since you hid him behind Mr Tran!

Lee is smiling. John takes him by the shoulders and they leave the office like two old friends. At the restaurant, Lee tells him the story of when he arrived in the US with his friend Bert Coldman. Bert held his promise: he introduced him to his family who welcomed him as a son, since he had saved theirs. He became a partner in the architect practice. He started doing research to find his family and became addicted to his work to try to forget the war and fill the gap in his life. Bert did everything to help him blend in; he managed to have his name Americanized as Lee Tran. Bert introduced him in his business circle. Very quickly, Lee won major contracts thanks to his skills, which confirmed his talent instead of being a 'protégé.' Three years later, the Coldman family went through a tragedy: Bert killed himself in his car with his young bride, as they were driving to their honeymoon. He was an only child. His parents suddenly behaved differently towards Lee. Bert's mother drew apart from him, unconsciously angry at him for being alive, whereas her darling son was dead. As for Bert's father, he gave him increasing responsibilities within the company, making him his official successor, but although professional relationship between the two men seemed to be fine, they emotionally grew apart day after day. Lee understood that he was not welcome anymore in their house. He felt betrayed and humiliated and worked even harder to compensate his disappointment. Five years later, the turnover doubled, when Coldman had a stroke and became paralysed. Since then, Lee was the only master in the most successful architectural firm in California. The Coldmans still held most of the shares, had a seat at the board meeting, but did not want to have anything to do with the life of the company. The only meeting they had with Lee was strictly for business. He had lost his American family, his hopes, and his illusions. This made him wants to reconnect with his roots and find his family, wife and children. He had wealth and could afford the best lawyers and investigators. For him, it was a question of revenge against fate. John Polsky learned more in one evening than in months of weekly sessions.

From this day, Lee Tran's therapy made great progress. He decides to get ready for the next vacation he will spend with his sons and enrols to a French intensive course. He reads plenty of books about France: its culture, its history, and its regions. It is for him a long and difficult path. He confessed: his father was a government official for the French colony administration, but those he admired and trusted were unable to defend the country during World War II. The Japanese occupation had been terrible, his disappointment was even greater. After the war, he joined the rebels and transmitted to his son his anger against the French. Lee has to overcome the prejudice with which he was raised, considering the French as the enemy. Worried to go against his father's education, he remembers little by little why his father went to Paris to study and loved in the first place what he came to hate later. He realized also that in France, the farmers are respected. He discovers that they have been free for centuries and do not compare with the poor coolies who were more slaves than men in the Vietnamese fields. Through his studies, he realizes that he considered his sons' adoptive parents by an old biased hatred and unfounded despise.

Despite the general 'ban' to develop personal relationship with a patient, John invests emotionally in his friendship with Lee. They discover together French restaurants in Los Angeles, learn how to appreciate good wines, listen to Joe Dassin, Gilbert Becaud, Charles Aznavour, Jacques Brel music... John advises him on books about adolescents. Lee Tran is transformed: he learns again how to laugh, to live, to appreciate the warmth of friendship. He changes his values.

CHARTRES, MARCH 1986

Marie-Claire has gained back enough strength to travel alone by train to Chartres where she has to go through new exams in the hospital before the congregation can decide whether she can go back to Vietnam. A few days later, she calls:

-I am fine, thanks to you, there is no more infection, but the doctors do not let me go yet. I need to stay at the motherhouse at least until June.

-I hope you can come see us, otherwise, we will arrange to come up.

-Thanks Mom. See you son.

Heart's bonds

July 1986, Lee's trip

Lee decides to perfect his French and become used to the country before he has to face what he is most afraid of: that his sons reject him again. The children are in a little village in the Black Mountain, in Saissac, near Carcassonne. With John, Lee prepared the trip: first, he will spend a few days to discover Paris, which he did not take the time to visit during his first two trips; then he will rent a car, travel down the Chateaux in the Loire Valley, cross the Dordogne region, then go down to Carcassonne. The books he read aroused his interest as an architect and he wants to make sure that he draws as many monuments, chateaux, manors as possible, which could inspire him later in his projects for his billionaire clients in Beverly Hills.

What he discovers is so much greater than what he has imagined, because no picture, no CD-Rom can show the magical beauty of the place. He is amazed, captivated, and happy. He feels like a child visiting Santa Claus workshop. His only regret is that John is not with him. He, Lee, the forever solitary, regrets for the first time that his friend is not sharing the simple joy of discovering France together.

He loves Paris, praises its magnificence, stays in the Loire's Chateaux, thinks of the plans for a smaller Azay-le-Rideau... When he discovers the Dordogne area, the old cities, the fortified towns, he is fascinated by the architecture of the 11th and 13th century. He would like to stay longer and find out about all the treasures the place has to offer, however, he keeps his promise to John and goes on as planned. He enjoys the sweet warmth and the quietness of Toulouse, the 'pink city', wishes to stay longer but takes the road to Carcassonne, divided between joy and panic at the idea of seeing his sons again and the welcome they will have for him.

The Martins rent out rooms; he decides to take one, booking at the same time a hotel room at the Best Western in Saissac, in case things turn out bad. He wishes to observe the way of life of his sons in the farm as well as their relationship with their adoptive family. He does not despise them anymore, he does not consider them as 'children thieves', he wants to find out what kind of a man and woman they are.

He leaves the highway at Castelnaudary to enter the Cathare country. He read books about the crusades against the Albigeois, his thoughts flow from the ancient drama and his own, between the remote past and this so unreal present...

When he arrives in Saissac, he has no difficulty finding La Ferme Haute, so called because the Martins' property stands at the high point of the town, overhanging the horizon and the ruins of the old castle. He parks in the farmyard. Louis stands in front of the door, plucking ducks. Lee, heartsick, forces a smile.

-Bonjour, I am Lee Tran.

-I know, answers Louis still working. He is a farmer of undefined age, tan with sun, wrinkled by hard work, round and heavy, imposing ... but there is an infinite sweetness in his eyes, some shrewdness at the corner of his lips when he smiles. Of course, he recognizes Lee Tran. How could he forget this man, surrounded by law men and interprets, haughty and cold, who came to take the 'little ones', without even asking them if they wanted to go, without a kind word or a thank you for those who raised them for ten years? This man who tried to dirty them in front of the judge so that he could take them. Does he believe that one adopts children out of interest? Cannot he fathom that it was out of love that they kept the pitchouns before he came as the 'father'? No, Louis has not forgotten his Simone's tears when she believed that she would never see them again, neither how skinny Benoît had been when he returned from America and the way the child held on to him saying: 'Daddy Louis, don't ever let him take me away again.'

Without showing it, Louis observes Lee. 'this time, he is alone, he booked a room ... what is he planning?' Louis has the suspicion of a peasant, but also that sixth sense that makes him feel danger, the aggressivity of people or any form of fear. He is foremost a brave man and after judging the man in front of him, he decides to stand up.

-Come on, I will show you your room.

-Where are the children?

-As usual, they are wandering around; you

will see them at dinnertime.

The first few days are difficult for Lee. His sons are avoiding him, he feels foreign; he is treated politely but more coldly than the other guests are. Used to luxury and space, his room seems tiny and strict. He feels ill at ease during the meals he takes at the house restaurant. All these strangers interacting as if they had known each other forever only because they are spending a few days under the same roof amazes him. Each time that one of them talks to him, he does not know how to react. Regularly, someone refers to his 'sons', the family resemblance being obvious. His heart sinks and does not answer.

He tries to speak French, gathers documents about the farm life, about the area. He finds out that La Ferme Haute is a small but real business, not only a guesthouse, but also a tin artisanal factory: foie gras, duck meat, casseroles, mushrooms, truffles, vegetables; with a store, the horse and pony rides and horse riding classes. It is a whole little world keeping busy under the leadership of Simone who seems to be the master of the house. She is the exact opposite of an 'iron hand in a velvet glove': she screams, she shouts orders, she seems to be bossing everyone but when looking more closely, you see that none of them is afraid of her; on the contrary, they all admire her because behind her Southern style she hides a woman attentive to everyone's comfort, treating those who work on the farm, in the kitchen, in the rooms with firmness but also with the tenderness of a mother demanding but just. She works hard too, ready to explode in seconds but it never lasts. Louis' calmness brings a great balance to the household, which shows unity through hundred little signs, saying much about their complicity, hiding the depth of their feelings only by decency.

Lee notices that his sons adore Didier. In spite of his fear of horses, he decides to take lessons. Didier chooses a docile mare and shows much patience. Quickly, Lee feels his fear vanish. He takes no pleasure in riding but he enjoys having his sons look at him during the class. Little by little, distrust is replaced by acceptance. Louis and Didier are the first to help Lee integrate the life of the household. The children have stopped fleeing him, even Simone seems to soften. One evening, some guests talk about the medieval festivities in Carcassonne and Lee offers to take the boys.

-I will only go if Didier goes, answers Benoît quickly.

-Don't be so difficult, Benoît, you know that Didier has to work, replies Louis.

Nothing else is said about it. Lee goes to bed wondering whether Pascal will accompany him the following day. In the morning, he is pleasantly surprised to find the two boys ready, apparently pleased to go. He has no idea what Louis told them but he is thankful anyway.

The city of Carcassonnes amazes Lee. It is a true gem and the three of them do three times the visit of the castle. Luckily, the boys share his enthusiasm. Most of all they love the medieval shows. Benoît, the 'yellow knight', is running towards the city wall. Unfortunately, his foot slips and he falls three feet down. When he stands and starts staggering, he is full of blood. Lee and Pascal run to him at the same time as a young woman.
-I am a doctor; let me look at him... Nothing serious, just a bad cut on his scalp. He bleeds a lot but a few stitches will be enough. Come with me, my office is close by.

Lee carries Benoît and follows the young woman. Pascal notices immediately the

little girl with her:
-Hello, my name is Christelle. She is my mother. What is your name?

When they arrive at the office, Christelle takes Pascal to the living room. Children have that wonderful ability to trust quickly and those two apparently have a thousand things to tell each other...

-I am Doctor Agnès Tournier. Are you Vietnamese?
-No, I am French; the sir here is American, answers Benoît, leaving Lee voiceless.
-Don't worry; I will give you a shot, so that it will not hurt anymore.

Lee looks at her. She is calm, her hand is steady. She is sweet and her voice soothes Benoît... She is also beautiful, with long red and curly hair and hazelnut eyes.
-Alright, it is all done, sweetheart. You can sleep for a little while, then I will give you something to eat. If everything goes well,

you should be up and running in time for the tonight show. She turns to Lee: He will probably sleep for an hour or so. May I offer you some tea or anything else in the meantime?

-I do not want to bother you. I can stay in the waiting room.

-Please accept my offer, I am on vacation; every year, I take a few days during the Medieval festival. Although we live in the city, we never get tired of it.

They have some tea, talk about Carcassonne... Doctor Tournier could go on forever about the history of the city and about its architecture, which surprises Lee. He is almost sorry to hear Benoît wake up. He offers to pay for the care and leave.

-Don't even think about it, you do not owe me anything. It was a pleasure to talk with an architect.

-In that case, may I invite you, your husband and your daughter for dinner, as a thank you for your help?

-I am a widow. However, from Christelle's laugh in the living room, I believe that she will be happy that we join you for dinner tonight.

One hour later, Benoît is running down the street with his brother and their new friend. The dinner is joyful, the night show is fantastic. They leave each other, promising to meet again.

The children fall asleep in the car as the engine starts, taking them back to La Ferme Haute. Lee thinks about Agnès Tournier. He was never particularly attracted to women. He likes neither the submission of Asian women, nor the aggressiveness of the Americans. He tried both, but only established superficial relationships. The only one who ever mattered to him was his sons' mother... he was so young, such a long time ago... Tonight, he can barely sleep. Doctor Tournier is educated, brilliant, jovial, confident but also calm, discreet (she made no allusion or remark about Benoît's comment, which probably sounded strange)... Lee finally fell asleep and slept about red hair mermaids...

The following day, Agnès and Christelle come to the farm for a horse ride. When she hears that Lee cannot go outside the corral, she decides to stay with him.
-Let the children go and we can take a walk...

This is how Lee learns that Agnès has been a doctor in Vietnam, in the Médecins Sans Frontieres (Doctors without borders) team. She knew the horror of war; the terrifying attack of Saigon, her husband died there, also a doctor... She can understand so much without saying anything...

They end up seeing Agnès and Christelle almost every day during the vacation. The children get along wonderfully, do races, have fun and laugh all the time. Pascal secretly told Yannick that even though he will always love Betsy, he thinks now that he would rather marry Christelle. So please, do not court her! He makes him promise to tell no one. Cross my heart, once everything is settled between them, they go and start playing the four musketeers.

From now on, the boys do not mind going with their father, and Yannick goes with them. They go back to Carcassonne several times, go to the different beaches of the area, most times meeting Agnès and Christelle there. Little by little, Pascal and Benoît change their minds about their father, without saying anything. At first, they said 'Sir', like in the US, but little by little, they start saying 'Father.' He sure still seems a little strange, but he is no longer the enemy. Since he is always willing to buy ice creams, go to the pizzeria or even fast food, the boys' friends find him 'cool.' Although Pascal and Benoît still feel ambivalent about him, they admit that he has changed completely from last year. Is that because he is in France, on vacation? Is it because of Agnès, so pleasant, smiling and full of life? Does he love them in his own way? The two brothers observe him. Their wish to be loved is stronger than their resentment and they start making efforts too. Weeks after weeks, their relationship improves.

Lee makes progress in horse riding, in French and he grows a passion about medieval architecture and restoration of historical monuments. He does not see how time flies by and discovers with great sadness that his last day of visit has come. That evening, Simone invites Agnès and Christelle, keeps Yannick for dinner and surpasses herself in cooking. Lee feels accepted, 'with a family.' He leaves and promises to write to everyone.

Los Angeles, Coming home

John is waiting for him at the airport.

-I have discovered a new French restaurant ... he starts.

-No, not tonight, let us eat Vietnamese!

Lee tells him about his stay, his discoveries, his disappointments, his fear, and then the slow and difficult task of being accepted... He talks about Carcassonne, Agnès...

-Oh My! You are in love! John shouts out, hearing him recite the thousands qualities of the latter.

-Of course not, you are a crazy old sentimental. I think highly of her, that is all.

John just smiles and swings on his chair, which for him says a lot about what he thinks about Lee's trying to defend himself. 'Here is a subject on which we will have pleasant therapy sessions', he wanders.

SEPTEMBER 1986, LA FERME HAUTE

After six months at the motherhouse, Sister Marie-Claire feels much better but the doctors advise her to take an extra month of rest before going back to Vietnam. This time, she can drive to her family. Her godsons are at school when she arrives. Louis and Simone went out to do errands. Didier is giving a class. He leaves his students to welcome his sister. They have become very close during the months of convalescence last winter. At 21, the young man seems much older. He passed his exams and is both graduated to teach horse riding and to be a guide for horse tours. Pony trek has become very trendy, for either a few hours or a few days. La Ferme

Heart's bonds

Haute is as well known in that field now, as it is in lodging and cuisine. Clients come from as far as Toulouse or Castelnaudary to take lessons. The stables have been extended and welcome horses in livery. Louis, proud of his son, gives him freedom to make his mark.

-How nice to see you in good shape again! You have no idea how you scared us at Christmas.

-Of course I do. I also thought it was the end of me. Fortunately, all of this is over now.

-I am going to have you work; I have two mares ready to give birth, too many students to have free time and six more weeks before the end of the season.

-That will be my pleasure. I hope I have not forgotten everything.

-I trust you on that. Let me drop your suitcase. Make yourself comfortable, I need to go back to the paddock. Come as soon as you can.

Marie-Claire puts on jeans, a sweater and her boots. She is going out of the house when everyone arrives. After many hugs, she manages to leave them and walk to her brother. Simone and Louis have a hard time forcing the boys to do their homework before going to the stables.

Almost every guest room is full. The whole family helps to prepare and serve dinner. After that, Pascal and Benoît must go to bed because tomorrow is a school day. Marie-Claire goes with them. They all sit on Benoît's bed.

-Finally alone! Come now; tell me about your father's visit. I heard Mom's version, you told me a little bit by phone, but now I want to hear what you think about it.

-He is not the same man who was in Los Angeles. He looks the same but this one speaks French and tries to be nice.

-Nonsense, Benoît! Of course, he is the same, he has changed, that's all.

-I do not believe it; I told you already, it is not possible!

-Benoît, why don't you think he changed? Don't you think that someone can become better? We all prayed a lot for that.

-Not me, I just wanted him to disappear.

-It is not nice to have such ideas.

-And you think what he did to us was nice?

-Forgive him, you have to understand him. And most of all, you must appreciate all the efforts he made to learn French so that he could talk to you.

-And to talk to Agnès! The boys giggle.

-Who is that?

-She is my friend Christelle's mother, continues Pascal, he spent more time with her than with us, but it worked fine for us.

-We will talk about it later. Now, it is getting late. Let us pray together and you go to bed.

Marie-Claire joins her mother in the kitchen.

-Sit down, I am making tea. You came here

to rest.

-Thanks Mom, but I am all right, do not worry. Who is this woman, Agnès, my godsons told me about?

-She is a fine person. She is a doctor, but very humble and easy. Last summer, she came almost every day from Carcassonne so that her daughter would improve her riding. A young and pretty girl, who Pascal is crazy about. He thinks I do not see it but it is so obvious. Can you believe it, he is fourteen and already playing Romeo!

-What about Dad and you, how old were you when it started?

-No, that is not the same; we were engaged when we were three, in kinder garden! Believe me or not, but I never looked at another boy in my life, as for your father, had he shown any interest in another girl, I would have ripped his eyes off.

The two women start laughing at the joke.

-You seem very cheerful, both of you, notices Louis as he enters the kitchen, what are you talking about?

Heart's bonds

-About Pascal looking at Christelle with loving eyes!

-He has good taste, she is very cute. If I were a few years younger, I would court her too.

-That would be the last straw! Do you want me to rip your heart off?

Hearing laughers, Didier comes to join them.

-Can I laugh too?

-Hey, you are a young man; tell your sister what you think of Christelle.

-She is a lovely girl. She rides beautifully; she could be a competition winner. Plus, she is very polite; always smiling never hesitates to grab a fork and help clean the stables... What is so funny about her?

-Haven't you noticed how Pascal looks at her lovingly?

-Of course, this one is no loyal chap: last year, he was dying of love for his American and this year, he is burning for another one. Far from the eyes, far from the heart, as we say, but at his age, he should be. He could fall in love a dozen times before finding the right one!

-Why do you say that? Your father and I found each other right away!

-And if I were loyal to my first love in pre-school, I would be with Josette, that silly cow who did not even make it to middle school.

Everyone laughs.

-It is so good to be with you, but I am getting tired, goodnight everyone.

The following Sunday, Agnès and Christelle come, as usual. After having lunch at the guest table, the children go for a horse ride. Agnès stays to talk with Sister Marie-Claire. They talk about different things. Agnès is curious to know how the situation became after the war and talks about her memories. The two women share the same love for the Vietnamese country and its people and very quickly, they feel close.

-I admire you for dedicating your life like

this, to see you so full of joy and enthusiasm in spite of all the difficulties.

-You know, it is easy, enthusiasm means: God with you!

-I know, alas I lost my faith when I was 14. My family had planned to spend the weekend by the ocean; I chose to stay in Carcassonne for a friend's birthday. They all died in a car crash: my parents, my sister and my little brother. I stopped believing in a loving God, who is interested in human fate. I felt guilty and was ashamed to be alive. I lived with my grandparents. I chose to become a doctor and intended to go far away to help the most unfortunate people. A little bit like a penance. I met my husband in Vietnam; we worked for the same Non Governmental Organization. He was Swiss and helped me find peace, thanks to his almost caricatured calm. With him, I had the impression that nothing bad could happen to me anymore. We had Christelle and in spite of the war, the difficult life conditions, I was finally happy. He was killed in a terrorist attack one week before Saigon fall. We went back to Lausanne with his coffin; our daughter was a little more than two. My in-laws wanted to keep us, but I felt the need to go back to Carcassonne, I thought that finding my roots would help me. It did not. I was too hurt, I could not bear my old friends, and I thought they could not understand me. I clanged to my daughter, opened a medical office, and became a workaholic, as we say.

-Christelle is a great teenager, full of life, of joy, you did a miracle, many children in her case are self-conscious.

-Thanks, it is true, she is radiant! She has a passion for horses, so here of course it is heaven for her. Life is sometimes strange; do you know that we met Lee by pure chance?

-Yes, the children told me.

-You see, there is something that few people know: many people who have cancer divorce, especially when they are in remission. Of course, sometimes, the spouse who had trouble facing the illness is sick and leaves tired, feeling that the healing allows him or her to go; but this is not the main reason. Most often, it is the sick person who leaves. He or she feels misunderstood, the spouse only living the other side of the picture, while only the experience of this fight against death can make one understand. I saw men and women finding a partner in chemo room, because two is stronger than one. For me, it was a little bit the same; I thought that I would never find someone able to understand what I had been through and how these hardships could make me both terribly fragile but also terribly strong. I sometimes feel like schizophrenia, one side of me taking care of the other.

-I understand that feeling perfectly.

-When I met Lee, I met a man who suffered even more than I did. He did not have the chance to go back to his country with his child. I know the Asian culture and I was able to guess the hidden treasures behind the mask, feel his great need to gain both the love and trust of his sons, all the while having great difficulties to express his feelings. I wanted to help him, to help them.

-It seems like you managed it very well.

-Marie-Claire, I never trusted anyone with this as I do with you just now. I understand the admiration your godsons have for you, you are a remarkable woman.

-Thank you, but let us not exaggerate; I am just trying to live in harmony with my faith.

-Knowing you, makes one want to believe in God.

-This is the nicest compliment I ever heard. Thank you Agnès, this is what I wish for you from the bottom of my heart. If I can help you trust God again, I would be very happy.

-Well, to start with, after spending time with the three boys, Christelle reproached me not to have signed her up for catechism and asks me to be baptized.

-What did you answer?

-Since she wants to, I contacted our Parish. She is starting a two-year course. If she does not change her mind until then, she will be baptized.

-Do you know what is said about chance? It is a miracle where God wants to stay incognito.

In the evening, taking advantage of being alone, Simone asks her daughter:

-What on earth did you have to talk about for so long with Agnès? You spent the whole afternoon like two conspirers.

-I listened to her. What do you think about her relationship with the boys 'father?

-They were together all the time. We could have thought something was going on between them, but we did not see any sign of affection, not once. We wondered, with your dad, if she would book a room one night, you are a nun, but you know what I am talking about, right? Well, nothing. In spite of all the miles, every night, she drove back to Carcassonne. With the team of four who spied on them all day, they could not take a chance of intimacy. So, what do you want me to think about it?

-Oriental people are much more reserved than occidentals are. To them, respect is more important than desire. If a man is in love, he is less likely to start a romance.

-Why is that?

-Because deep feelings can only be expressed through a marriage proposal. If circumstances make the union improbable, then nothing will be ever said or shown.

September goes by fast, it seems like Marie-Claire has just arrived and already she must go. She had a confirmation that she was flying to Vietnam in two weeks. It will be both a great joy to see her sisters and the children again, but also a sadness to leave her family. The months spent with her family brought them back all together, once more showing her the price of her sacrifice: *'Anyone who loves their father or mother or brother more than me is not worthy of me....'*

Saying 'yes' again, giving again and again her heart and her life. The nun looks lovingly at her family who gathers around her before she goes. She remembers that month of June 1975 when she left her godsons to her parents. She feels the same lump at her throat, the same knot at her stomach. She holds her tears. Just like she did eleven years ago, she knows that she has done the right choice. She hurries to start the engine, waves with her hand and lets her tears run down her face.

DECEMBER 1986, LOS ANGELES

-Although you are a nasty person who does not believe in him,Santa brought you a gift!

John, smiling, puts a book on the restaurant table where Lee is waiting for him on this December 26th.

-'*Men come from Mars, women from Venus*', what should I do with it?

-This is the new bestseller about relationships between men and women. A funny little guide about how we can understand the fundamental differences that often bring issues.

-You are forgetting that I was married and I have known a few women in my life!

-Don't take it so lightly. Trust me; you are

going to need this.

-Are you a fortuneteller now? An extra lucid psychiatrist?

-If what I wish for you from the bottom of my heart happens, read this book and you will thank me later.

-Don't tell me you believe in stereotypes and clichés whose only goal is to make people laugh. I have been to France and I have not seen one man wearing a beret and carrying a baguette under his arm!

-Touché! Nevertheless, there is always something true in legends. So please, be kind to me, put your type A brain at rest and we will talk about it later. I am hungry, let us order.

The two men do not meet in John's office anymore; the behavioural therapies, contrary to analysis, are short. Because they are friends, they are used to having dinner at least once a month and enjoy these moments of friendship. Because of his job, John cannot help himself from giving books to Lee, which, he thinks, will help him in his evolution. Lee is well aware of that, but plays along out of respect for his friends' care but also because he finds the books very interesting.

-I brought you a gift too, in fact, a double gift because it is for both of us.
-Tell me now.
-I have two seats for *'In the Name of the Rose.'* Let us have a quick meal, it starts at 10.
-Well, it seems like we are not leaving the Medieval Age!

As months are going by, Lee Tran becomes a different person. Any building less than a few centuries old seem of no interest to him, his construction projects look like old houses from the South west of France, he only reads in French, contributes to the association 'Doctors With No Border.' He joined a gym, goes to the pool, and avoids the jet set parties, which for years used to bring him so many clients. Realizing that the result of his new behaviour induces a drop in turnover, he looks among his employees the three most likely to help him on projects, sales and management. He discovers how great it is to delegate and to establish relationship based on trust at work. Very soon, the sales go up again and he can go back to his new favourite activities without jeopardizing his company.

Quickly, Agnès and Lee exchanged increasingly kind letters, learning more about each other, sharing their thoughts... Christelle being passionate about horses is a good reason to visit the boys each week and create bounds with them, never missing an opportunity to say something pleasant about their father. She has become the man's 'ambassador' to the boys and their French family... In the same way, Lee learns more about his sons through Agnès' letters than through the short messages written by them. Pascal writes regularly, and little by little, Benoît adds a few words to his brother's letters. They talk about school, anecdotes about their children lives...

EASTER 1987, LA FERME HAUTE

Today is April 19, 1987, Easter Day; Pascal is celebrating his fifteenth birthday. Although he knows now that he was born on February 24th, he insists on having his birthday party on Easter Day. It is also Benoît's Communion. Simone and Louis invited Yannick's family, the Lerasle, Isabelle and her husband, as well as Agnès and Christelle. Father Emmanuel also came to comfort Benoît that his godfather and godmother could not come. He is very disappointed about that but does not want to show anything to Mommy Simone: she has done so much to prepare an unforgettable feast that he does not want her to be sad.

Since school started, the children have changed much. Of course, they all have grown. The voices of Yannick and Pascal have changed at about the same time and they start to have some hair above their lips; they regularly pretend they need to shave and both fathers play along while both mothers look up at the sky, sorry to see them leave childhood and become teenagers. Yannick is about a head taller than Pascal, but Pascal does not mind because he is very happy to be much taller than Benoît now, after having his little brother closely following him for years. The two teenagers have started high school and for the first time since kindergarten are no longer in the same class. This does not keep them from challenging each other to be the best student, which pleases their parents. Benoît is in seventh grade and takes advantage of his English skills, well ahead of his fellow pupils, to win a prize for his general grades. However, among the 'four musketeers', Christelle is the one who changed most. At fourteen, she seems eighteen, showing curves, letting imagine the beautiful woman she will be one day. She got rid of her tumble boy character and exchanged it for makeup and a trendy teenage look. To Pascal despair, she grew up more quickly than he grow and is now the size of Yannick.

The ceremony is beautiful. The sky, grey in the morning, lets the rainfall during the service and gave place to a beautiful blue sky when everyone went out. At La Ferme Haute, the meal is served in the covered courtyard. Not only is each dish delicious and generous, but there are two desserts: a birthday cake for Pascal (his favourite: a raspberry cake with almond crust) and a pièce montée for Benoît. During the gift distribution, surprises from the US are distributed: a golden watch for Pascal and one for Benoît, but also a watch for Yannick and one for Christelle; a necklace for Simone and one for Agnès, a pair of riding gloves for Didier and one for Louis. There are also five boxes of See's Candies: toffee and Californian chocolates the boys enjoyed during their visit. More than the gifts, it is the fact that Lee thought of each one of them that touched everyone. For the first time, Pascal and Benoît regret that their father is not here in person to share that day with them.

Heart's bonds

MAY 1987, LOS ANGELES

Gleaming of joy, Lee announces to his friend his great decision after thinking about it for a long time:

-John, I decided to take a sabbatical year. I want to go to Paris, take a class at the Beaux-Arts* and study the techniques to restore historical monuments.

-Is that not too far from Carcassonne? Asks John, with a wink.

-Less far than Beverly Hills! I told my sons and their family about my project and they all encouraged me, they think it is a great idea.

*Most famous art school in France

-All of them, men and women?

-You will not leave me alone will you!
Give me some time to settle and then come
for a visit me in France. I will be your
guide.

-I am your man, and actually also your
'best man'!

-You are incurable!

Heart's bonds

Only the details need to be arranged: his visa, the enrolment to his class, the management of his company while he is gone, the organization of his trip, but also his vacation is Saissac. A few weeks later, the two friends meet again.

-Ready? How do you feel?
-I went to the Coldman to take care of a few legal issues. I had the feeling that they did not care about my leaving for France, the only thing that interested them was the guarantee that business would be taken care of. With only 60% of the assets, they receive today more than double, what they earned 12 years ago when I joined the company and they had 100% of the shares. You see, one year ago, I would have been devastated by their indifference to me and angry against their lack of gratitude. Today, I do feel nostalgic about the years they welcomed me into their family, and it still

hurts to think about the tragic death of Bert and his wife, but I do not feel directly involved anymore. I do not know if I am making myself clear.

-You finally understand that you are not responsible for their feelings towards you. You do not feel guilty to be alive anymore. It is wonderful!

-Yes, you are right; I have never felt this 'alive.'

-And you finally allow yourself to be happy.

-I promise you to try.

Heart's bonds

La Ferme Haute, June 1987

Today June 7th, Pascal and Yannick have their Confirmation. Again, Father Emmanuel came to replace the boy's godfather, bishop Benoît, who had to stay in his diocese for the Pentecost celebration.

-Well, am I going to have two godfathers now? Asks Pascal, trying to cheer up and not be disappointed.
-If you accept me, I will be your Confirmation godfather and you will be spiritually supported twice as much, with a bishop and a priest to protect you and to guide you.
-Alright, I am good with that. I like you, you know.

-I like you too.

During the ceremony, Pascal walks down the aisle, Father Emmanuel's hand on his shoulder and he receives Confirmation by the Bishop of Toulouse.

The meal is grand, in the afternoon, everyone goes to the vespers. The evening is pleasant, daylight stayed until close to eleven. The temperature is just right; a small breeze brings some cool air and the smell of the fields.

Father Emmanuel invites Pascal for a little walk.
-You seem to be worried about something, less happy than on your birthday. Do you want to tell me what is going on?
-I do not know, it is not easy. Only my godfather knows my secrets.
-Am I not your godfather too, since this morning?
-Yes, of course, but won't you laugh at me?

-Promise.

-Have you seen how Christelle has changed?

-She is a lovely girl indeed.

-She is a year younger than I am but seems ten years older!

-You are exaggerating, two or three at the most. You know, boys and girls do not always grow at the same age. Is that what worries you?

-I am short but look at Yannick!

-He is taller than you are, which is normal, look at his father? However, what is wrong with that? You are a smart boy, you work well at school, you are sensible, and you ride as well as your friends. As for the looks, you are a handsome young man; the size really does not matter. Why are you so upset: you are taller than Benoît and still keep growing?

-Each time I fall in love, I have no luck.

-You are only fifteen; you have all the time in the world to find someone. Look at

Louis, he is not tall, but that did not keep him from marrying Simone.

-They are the same size, at least.

-Well, you see, you may find a girl your size one day or you may marry a girl a head taller than you and who cares about the difference, what matters is the soul, the spirit and the heart.

-I made Yannick promise me that he would not court Christelle, but she looks at me like a friend and at him with loving eyes.

-What does he think about it?

-He swore that he would not take her from me.

-But she is not yours! You cannot do that. If Yannick is your friend and if you really love Christelle, you need to let them free.

-If they kiss or hold hands in front of me, I would be sick.

-This is called jealousy. This is the opposite of love and friendship.

-I already gave up on Betsy, do I have to give up on Christelle too?

-If she is meant to be yours, she will come back one day. Be patient. Otherwise, it means that you will find a better fit later. When God does not answer one of our prayers, it is generally because He has a better idea.

-Do you think He wants me to become a priest?

-Only you can know.

-I would like to be a priest, but I also want to be married.

-Please explain.

-You are happy but Daddy Louis is too. You know, when they do not think we are looking at them, with mommy Simone, they exchange looks, which I can only understand now that I am in love. Even when Simone says: 'What have I done to the Lord to have such a husband?' I know that in fact, it is only because she is angry and she would not live without him for all the riches in the world.

-You are a good observer. You are right, I also think that those two are meant for each other and show exactly what the Bible say: *"A man will leave his father and mother and unite with his wife, and the two will become one."*

They stay quiet for some time.

-Father Emmanuel, have you been in love before becoming a priest?

-Of course, the first time, I was four, we were in Kindergarten, her name was Leslie and she tied my shoes. You see, I did not forget her, I even pray for her regularly and for all the little girls who tie the shoes of their friends.

-Alright, but seriously, when you were a young man like me?

-Like every boy, I have been in love several times. Each time we think it is for life, that we will die if she leaves us, that she is the only one worth loving, that no one has ever loved like us before or can understand.

-Yes, exactly. So they have all left you and you became a priest?

-Not exactly. It was not easy but I discovered that I loved Jesus more than anyone in the world, that He loved me so much that He gave His life for me, that He will always be there for me, I understood that my greatest joy was to follow Him, to love and serve Him.

Another silence.
-Have you ever thought about becoming an orthodox? You could get married and be a priest.
-I chose the vocation I was called for. I did not try to combine opposite desires; if I had really wanted to be married, I would have become a deacon.
-But it is not the same.
-No, it is a choice. You are still very young, Pascal, you have thousands of questions in your mind and it is good, but stop thinking, start feeling. Stop talking and start listening. In a few years, you will not hesitate anymore, you will know which path to take and why.

-Follow the example of my godfathers or Daddy Louis...

-Take YOUR path, the one you choose. Whichever it is, it will be the right choice for you. I trust you for that.

-Tomorrow, I will talk to Yannick.

-That is a good start, concludes Father Emmanuel smiling.

They come back in silence, the priest holding the young boy by the shoulder.

Heart's bonds

PARIS, JULY 1987

Lee arrives in Roissy on a sunny morning. Agnès is waiting for him. The letters have always remained friendly. Lee is now aware that his feelings for her go far beyond what he says. What about Agnès?

They exchange a fraternal kiss.
-Let me take you to your hotel, you must want to shower after a twelve hour flight.

She already has the keys to his room. Just like on the first day, she seems on top of everything, Lee just wants to let her lead and let himself go.
-Take a shower, I will order some Champagne. I have great news for you.

-What is it about?

-Be patient! Go, it is important to celebrate events, as they deserve, she adds smiling, pushing him lightly to the bathroom.

Curious and vaguely worried, Lee takes a shower and changes clothes. Clean and shaved, he shouts to her:

-Am I finally worthy of your confidence?

She smiles and starts:

-I found a friend I had known in Saigon.

At these words, Lee's heart stops beating. She goes on:

-He and his wife live in Paris.

Lee's heart starts beating again.

-He works for SOS Médecin* and offered me to join the association, they have great needs in Paris.

-You would leave Carcassonne to come here? Lee does not dare thinking what such a change would mean.

-That is, if a certain architect I know wishes me at his side, while he studies at the Beaux Arts... she adds smiling.

Association specialized in medical emergencies

Heart's bonds

Lee's heart is racing. He feels like a teenager with his first love. He wants to cry and laugh, sing on the roofs, stay mute... He takes her in his arms and becomes a lover who can finally touch the fruit of a long dream.

It takes three days and three nights to calm the wonderful storm that took over them. They discover each other, surprise each other, harmonize and rest, consume each other and catch fire. They take their shower together, use room service, and forbid the house cleaner to come inside. They love each other with passion, erasing all the years of solitude, the wounds of the past, the worries and the fear. They tame each other and amaze each other. They had never known such a passion. They have found each other and know that they will never separate. Agnès remembers something Marie-Claire told her: '*Chance is a miracle where God wants to stay incognito.*' She feels inside of her the lucidity of her childhood: 'and if it were true?'

Once they catch breath and decide to go out, Lee takes a cab to go to Place Vendôme. In front of the jewellery window, he smiles to Agnès.
-I need a ring to ask you to marry me, but I need your hand to choose a ring.
A kiss is her answer; he takes her by the hand and enters the jewellery.

They take the long road to drive down to Saissac. They need a few more days to reinforce their happiness and feel ready to talk to their children.

Heart's bonds

AUGUST **1987,** LA FERME HAUTE

Christelle stayed at La Ferme Haute while her mother was away. The 'four musketeers' watch out for the arrival of Lee and Agnès.

The car is barely parked, the kids run to greet them. Louis shakes hands with Lee with a large smile and gives a kiss to Agnès. Didier lets his trainees take care of their horses and comes to welcome them. Simone weaves from the kitchen, wipe her hands on her apron and starts pouring wine in glasses.

At this time of day, the guests are out. They all take place in the main room. Lee is relieved because Agnès cannot wait to tell the news.

-Lee and I are getting married...

Some 'yes, great, wonderful...' punctuate her sentence. Lee looks at Christelle, anxious, afraid at the idea that she may reject him, just like his own sons had done at first, but the young girl runs to him and says:

-Most important of all, make my mother happy, otherwise you are in trouble! She gives him a kiss, smiling.

-When are you getting married? Asks Pascal.

-As soon as possible, but it takes a few weeks to get all the paperwork done, arrange all the details, the ceremony and the party, invite the friends...

-Can we invite Betsy and Jack?

Lee is surprised by Pascal's request. Betsy. It all seems such a long time ago! It has only been two years... He rarely thought about the young woman who spoke as sharp as a surgeon scalpel... Although she had been the first one to link him back to life and urge him to change path...

-I don't believe that Betsy wishes to see me again and I don't have her address...

-I do. We still write to each other...

-In that case, I will be happy to treat her to a visit in France with no condition. She will come whenever she wants and she will not have to see me.

-No, she has to come for the wedding. I want her to see how you have changed.

-And do not forget Godfather and Godmother, adds Benoît, so happy at the idea of having everyone he loves gathered.

-You know how hard it is to have your godmother, says Simone, with great sadness in her voice.

-God has achieved a miracle, He could do another one, answers Pascal, confident.

Lee is moved by the answer of his son.

The two following weeks go by very

quickly, there is so much to do, so many details to arrange for... Lee and Agnès decide to drive to Paris to choose an apartment. The morning before they leave, Pascal asks:

-Are you taking Christelle to Paris, when you move there?

-Of course, why?

-Well, Benoît and I would like to go too, if that is all right, so when you choose an apartment, you need to find a room for us as well.

Lee is elated.

-It will be a great joy, but you are not yet sixteen. You will next year, Pascal, but Benoît is only twelve.

Louis starts talking:

-Well, you should know that Simone and I have been thinking about that for a while now. Since Agnès told us she was going to live in Paris, well, we are not stupid, you know, so we thought about it. If the boys wish to live with you, we will not keep them from doing so. However, at one condition of course: you will send the three of them for each school vacation, all three, because now Christelle is a member of the family, just as your future babies will, I hope.

He speaks from the bottom of his heart with all the kindness and the good judgement he is well known for.

-Let's celebrate then, I'm taking out the Blanquette de Limoux I put in the fridge for the occasion, adds Simone, who dries discretely the tears that form at the corner of her eyes; she does not want to spoil the boys' happiness by showing her sadness at seeing them 'fly away.' She knows that real love is to let someone choose his own happiness. Her 'little ones' will leave the nest sooner than expected, but this time for the best. She thinks of her daughter Christine, Sister Marie-Claire, and of her sorrow to leave the children behind, her recommendation: '*They are not ours and one day, they will go away...*' Yes, thinks

Simone, they belong to nobody except themselves, free to choose their own lives, even if it hurts.

Benoît feels the emotion of the adults and is not sure to understand what is going on exactly.

-So, are we going to live in Paris or not?

-A thousand times yes, answers Lee. He holds his sons against his heart. He has finally made it to the port.

THE END

Heart's bonds

ACKNOWLEDGEMENT

I want to thank my reading comity: Marie-Astrid Lemercier, Anne-Marie Visse, Emmanuel Benfenati, Laura Journault, Matthew Lambert, Geoffrey Jacob, Nelly Waysbaum, Marie-Michèle et Pascal de Sloover, Laurence Basta, Sylvie Lafont, for their encouragements and smart comments.

And thank you, unknown reader, who takes some of your precious time to share a moment with me. I hope it has been an interesting and pleasant experience.

May everyone draw here or there within the story, a bit of my soul, like a fraternal gift.

COMMENTS FROM THE AUTHOR

Les Sœurs de Saint Paul de Chartres, or The Sisters of Saint Paul of Chartres is a missionary congregation founded in 1696. Initially it was meant for the education of girls, visits to the poor and assistance to the ill. Today it exists in 35 countries on the five continents and serves 'the indigent, the poor, the excluded.' The order accounts for 4,000 sisters, from which 1,000 in Vietnam.

When they first arrive in Saigon in 1890, the sisters welcome the orphans and set up a hospital. Six years later, the novitiate opens its door to many Vietnamese women.

Heart's bonds

The Order develops and builds hospitals, schools and orphanages across the country.

After the fall of Saigon, all the buildings are nationalized. The sisters are only allowed to work in hospitals. Not until 1990 will, they be allowed to open schools again.

The story of this congregation inspired me greatly; however, the characters in my novel are completely fictive.

Saissac is a village in the department of Aude, surrounding the ruins of a beautiful Cathar castle. It lies in a triangle: Toulouse, Castelnaudary, Carcassonne. Do not look for 'La Ferme Haute', which only exists in my imagination. You will not find Simone or Louis either, but the people of that area inspired their characters to me, particularly dear to me. Do not hesitate to visit it, who knows what treasure you will discover!

Los Angeles: All right, I admit, Betsy is the name of one of my nieces who looks like her both physically and mentally, as an 'allusion to my fondness of her', the rest is pure fiction. I lived many years in California and left a bit of my heart there.

The children: they are a mixture of all the ones I love... They became alive as the novel progressed; I sometimes expect them to ring at my door...

Heart's bonds

ABOUT THE AUTHOR

Born in France, Pascale d'Harmat spent most of her life working abroad. Thirteen years in the USA, two in Canada, four years in several European countries. From her confrontation to different cultures, she has gained an open spirit, tolerance, curiosity and a large variety of experiences she loves to share.

Her work shows great spirituality and an optimist conception of life in spite of numerous hardships. Her desire to bring hope to a large number of people is why she chose to go public, after having shared her work in private circles for a long time.

Heart's bonds

Heart's bonds

SOON TO DISCOVER FROM THE SAME AUTHOR

Nazareth, the hidden years:

What did Jesus do between the age of 12 and the age of 30? What was his relationship with the Esséniens? Why was he called Rabbi? Who were his sister and brothers? What were their roles? How did Jesus live? Why did the people ask for the liberation of Barabbas? One day or another, you might have asked yourself, one or all of these questions and many others.

What no Gospel told us, Myriam, Jesus' sister, discloses in this novel where historical facts from Galilee and Judea one century after Christ mix with evangelical spirit and a good amount of imagination where plausible, possible and unknown meet for our greatest pleasure.

Pascale d'Harmat

Heart's Bonds
Translated by Agnès Rouvrais-Waysbaum

Printed by lulu.com
January 2012
Editions Claire Fontaine

ISBN 978-2-917734-60-5

Editions Claire Fontaine
6, rue des Petits Champs – 78360 Montesson
Siret 503 978 702 000 10
www.editions-claire-fontaine.com
contact@editions-claire-fontaine.com